DAWN LEE MCKENNA'S

DEAD WAKE

A *FORGOTTEN COAST* SUSPENSE NOVEL:
BOOK FIVE

2015

A SWEET TEA PRESS PUBLICATION

First published in the United States by Sweet Tea Press

Edited by Tammi Labrecque
larksandkatydids.com

Cover by Shayne Rutherford
darkmoongraphics.com

Interior Design by Colleen Sheehan
wdrbookdesign.com

Dead Wake is a work of fiction. All incidents and dialogue, and all characters, are products of the author's imagination. Any similarities to any person, living or dead, is merely coincidental.

For
Martin Sheen

Whose kindness and generosity
had a profound and lasting impact on a young writer

CHAPTER ONE

The dead guy was one of the few people around on Commerce Street that night.

Downtown Apalachicola, FL was quiet; the shops had all closed for the day, and most of the commerce was taking place at the cafes, restaurants, and raw bars that dotted the streets along the bay. The palm trees that punctuated the brick sidewalks danced in the October breeze, their fronds rustling like old newspaper.

At the florist on the corner, just a few blocks from the water, the windows were still lit, though the shop was closed to business. In the box windows, white Christmas lights cast their perkiness upon displays of bridal bouquets, fall wreaths, and birthday arrangements, and the faint sounds of Vivaldi could have been heard from the sidewalk, if anyone had been on it.

Inside the flower shop, William Overton unrolled sheet plastic on the floor behind the counter, kicking it along with his foot. Once the entire six by ten expanse of floor was covered, he cut the plastic sheeting with a box cutter and put the rest of the roll on the counter.

He and his partner, Robert Manetti, had removed the work counter that had been against the back wall, and Robert had just come back from Home Depot with aprons, dust masks, wood for building a new half wall/counter, and a handy-looking red sledgehammer they would probably have no use for ever again.

Now, while Robert brought the supplies in through the back door and put them in the back hallway, William stared at the wall they were about to vanquish. The bottom third of the sheetrock was badly stained and coming apart in small chunks. It had been damaged by the floodwaters caused by Hurricane Faye a couple of months prior, and the wall had been picking away at William's sanity since.

The insurance company had barely afforded them enough money to clean up the shop and replace the damaged floors and display cases. There was no money left to repair the wall that separated the front of the shop from a storage room in back, so William and Robert, armed with a selection of YouTube videos and years of experience watching HGTV, had had decided to do the work themselves.

William, who spent his limited patience sparingly, had begun picking at the damaged sheetrock that morning, and found there was brick behind it. Once he'd started picking, he'd been unable to stop, and had peeled away several feet of ragged sheetrock throughout the day. The mortar between the bricks was also crumbling and soft, and he'd chipped at it here and there with a tire iron, worrying it the way an old man would a sore tooth.

After considerable lip-pursing and nail-chewing, William had decreed that they should tear down the brick and remove the wall altogether, thus opening up the space nicely and bringing in more light. He'd allowed Robert enough time to hem but not quite enough to haw, and idea became plan forthwith.

William reached down and grabbed the handle of the sledgehammer, expecting to be able to sling it right out of the box in which it stood. The sledgehammer, however, refused to be slung by anyone as unimpressive as William, who stood about five-foot eight, weighed one hundred and forty pounds, and hadn't worked out since Richard Simmons was the king of fitness.

With notable effort, William dragged the sledgehammer out of the box, wrapped both hands around the handle, and attempted to bring it up like a baseball bat. He managed to lift it about four feet before it fell back to the concrete floor with a substantial *thunk*.

"What are you doing?' Robert called from the hallway.

"I'm getting everything ready," William called back, as he tried once more to lift the sledgehammer.

"Don't mess with anything," Robert said as he walked back toward the door that opened onto the alley. "I've got one more load to bring in from the van."

"I'm not messing with anything," William said, then grunted as the sledgehammer thumped to the floor a second time. "Oh, whatever," he muttered, and abandoned the idea of actually swinging the thing.

He changed his grip, arranged himself in a golfing stance, and teed off, tapping at the bottom of the exposed brick. A few crumbs of mortar fell to the floor. He put a little more attitude into his next swing, and managed to knock loose three bricks, about two feet up from the floor.

William's nose was immediately assaulted by a malodorous greeting from things wet and rotting, and he swallowed back a twinge of nausea as he held his nose shut for a moment. They'd been keeping Febreze in business for the last couple of months, trying to mask the growing odor of mold and damp and rot. However, what was coming through the hole in the wall was far more offensive. Determined to get the wall down and bleach the snot out of the whole area toot-sweet, William climbed atop a chair and then took a swing at a spot higher up.

At first, only a handful of bricks came loose, then several more above the hole they'd left. William hopped off the chair to survey his progress, kicking a few bricks out of his way. Then he stared into the hole he'd made, from which someone stared back at him.

Robert was coming through the back door when he heard William screech. William's was a distinctive scream, and it was generally employed only in extreme instances of injury or spider. Robert dropped the last bag from Home Depot in the hallway and hurried out to the front.

William was standing next to a chair, with a small collection of sheetrock and bricks around his feet and the sledgehammer hanging from his hand. He was staring at the wall as though they'd installed a flat screen there. He looked over at Robert as he rounded the corner.

"Look at this nonsense!" William spat out indignantly.

Robert came to stand next to William and looked at the hole his partner had made. It was narrow, but ran from just above the floor to about five feet up the wall. Robert couldn't help being impressed with his partner's progress, since William generally had trouble lifting a well packed carry-on.

There, in between two studs and behind two crossbeams, was someone who had seen better days. He'd been wrapped in some sort of clear plastic, but most of it had either rotted or fallen away from the head.

"Heavens to Mergatroid," Robert said quietly. "It's a dead guy."

William glared over at his partner of twenty-six years. "Of course it's a dead guy. We don't keep any living guys in our walls."

"It smells like a rat crawled into a dirty sock and died," Robert said. "We gotta open some windows before it smells up the whole shop."

"Are you deranged?" William asked as Robert hurried around the counter. "Then everyone that comes down the street will smell it!"

Robert stopped. "Well, what do you suggest?" he asked, one hand on his hip, the other covering his mouth and nose. "It'll take days to get that smell out of here. We'll have to close!"

"Hush up and let me think," William answered shortly, then looked beyond Robert to the front windows and let out a quick yelp.

"What?!" Robert looked over his shoulder at the front door.

"Close the blinds! Hurry up, before somebody sees."

William scurried around the counter to help Robert lower the bamboo blinds, although no one was likely to be out on Commerce Street. Then they returned to the back of the room, though they stayed on the other side of the counter this time. They stood there contemplating the wall for several moments.

Judging by the stiff and dusty Dickies overalls, the body appeared to be that of an unattractive man. It had slumped a bit at some point, and its knees, or what remained of its knees, were resting on the lower of the two beams in front of it.

"It's almost like he was praying," William said in a hushed tone.

"Well, it looks like God said 'no,'" Robert answered.

"This is very bad for business."

"Tragic even," Robert agreed.

They both stared in silence for another moment, then Robert shook himself. "I'm going back to Home Depot. We're gonna brick him right back up."

"Have you lost your mind?' William asked him, folding his arms across his chest.

"Why not?" Robert asked.

"Well, for one thing, we don't know how to lay brick," William answered.

"Neither did somebody else," Robert said, sweeping a hand at the wall. "Look at that crappy job. If a Gumby like you can take it down—"

"This is not the occasion for slurs," William snapped. "I will not have him here. I won't stand for it!"

"What would you like me to do, then? Put him out in the dumpster?"

"Call 911," William said.

"If you wanted the whole town to know our business, then why'd we close the stupid blinds?"

William huffed out a sigh and propped his fists on his hips. They stared at the dead guy some more.

"You're right," William said finally. "Forget 911. Go call the little sheriff."

⚓ ⚓ ⚓

Maggie Redmond disconnected the call and stared through her windshield at the front of Sheriff Wyatt Hamilton's sage-green cottage. The porch light reflected on the pavers leading to the front steps, the concrete still damp from a five-minute evening shower.

Through the open windows of her Jeep Cherokee, Maggie could hear the rustling of the palmettos on either side of the short gravel driveway. She sighed and tapped at Wyatt's number on her recent calls list.

"Hey, where are you?' Wyatt asked when the call connected.

"In your driveway," Maggie answered.

"Excellent. Next you get to come inside."

Maggie sighed. "I can't. I have to go."

"Usually you have to arrive before you can leave."

"I realize that," Maggie answered. "But William and Robert have a problem."

"The flower guys?"

"Yes. Something about finding Lon Chaney in their wall."

Maggie both watched and heard the front door open. Wyatt stood bathed in the light from his living room, wearing cargo shorts and a blue Hawaiian shirt, his cell phone at his ear.

"Junior or senior?" Wyatt asked her.

"They didn't specify."

"I'm pretty sure Lon Chaney's out in California," Wyatt said.

"Well, somebody dead, scary, and bad for business is in the wall at the flower shop."

"James is on duty. Why'd Dispatch give it to you?"

"They didn't. Robert called me himself."

She could see Wyatt roll his eyes. "Did he forget the number for 911?" he asked.

Maggie gave Wyatt an exasperated face through her windshield. "Are you coming or not?"

She heard the sigh as she watched the shoulders slump.

"Yeah, yeah. Let me put real shoes on."

Maggie hung up and watched him slip out of his flip flops and slide his feet into Docksiders, then close the door and head down the walkway toward her Jeep.

At six-four, Wyatt was imposing, but his loose-limbed gait, somewhat goofy sense of humor, and laughing eyes made him a favorite among the locals, both men and women. He'd been shot just a few months previously, and had undergone surgery and physical therapy for his hip, but he'd recently been able to give up his cane, and had only the slightest of limps.

Wyatt was Maggie's boss at the Sheriff's Office. Over the years he had become her closest friend and, over the last few months, something else they had yet to define.

He opened the passenger door and slid in, then slammed the door shut. "May I explain to you all of the ways that this event will not enhance our date?"

Now it was Maggie's turn to roll her eyes. "Sure, why not?"

"Well, first of all, I wasted two hours this afternoon putting together the perfect slow dancing playlist on Spotify."

"That's sweet."

"Yes, it was," Wyatt said. "Additionally, there will no doubt be much less kissing at the flower shop than there would have been on my back patio."

"No doubt." Maggie stared back at Wyatt, who had raised his rather impressive eyebrows at her. "What? Are you expecting me to take some kind of responsibility for the fact that the flower guys have a dead body in their shop?"

"No, but I would like you to feel badly about the playlist."

"I feel exceptionally bad about the playlist. What's on it?"

"Well, some Civil Wars for one thing."

"I love The Civil Wars."

"I know you do. I also threw a little Ella Fitzgerald in there."

"The big guns."

"Precisely. And now it's all for naught, since I generally do very little slow dancing at crime scenes."

"Please accept my apology," Maggie said.

"I would prefer not to," Wyatt answered. "Why don't I just call James and have him check it out? It's his shift."

"No." Maggie sighed and her shoulders slumped a little. "I'm sorry, but I told them I would come."

Wyatt stared at Maggie, and the frankness in his eyes made her suddenly aware of the smallness of the car, the faint scent of his cologne, and the slight tingling sensation in her chest.

"Well," he said quietly, suddenly far more serious. "Then we should go ahead and have a nice kiss now."

"We should," Maggie answered. That tingling in her chest intensified as she watched Wyatt lean toward her. Once his mouth pressed onto hers, gently but firmly, the tingling was replaced by an odd pairing of peace and excitement. Maggie closed her eyes and fell into it, and experienced a feeling not unlike that of the first day in a new home.

After a moment, Wyatt pulled away and sighed, then broke the tension with a wink. "I bet right about now you're wishing you'd let that call go to voice mail. As you should, on your way to a date."

"I would love to have done that, but I didn't," Maggie answered. "Now I feel obligated to handle it. They're pretty put out."

"I'm a little put out, too," he said.

"I know. The playlist."

"And the salad."

"You made a salad?" Wyatt's favorite vegetable was Doritos. The fact that he'd handled produce was notable.

"Well, no. But I had a heck of a time opening the bag."

Maggie shook her head and smiled as she shifted into reverse. "You're such a toddler."

"Am not."

W hen Maggie and Wyatt parked at the curb in front of the flower shop, the blinds were uncharacteristically shut and there was a "Closed" sign on the front door. Wyatt rapped on the door and, a moment later, fingers separated the blinds on the door and a pair of anxious eyes peered out at Wyatt and Maggie. A few seconds later, Robert opened the door.

"Hurry, come in," he said in a near-whisper. He rushed them through the door, then closed and locked it. He and Wyatt raised their eyebrows at each other as Robert took in the Hawaiian shirt and cargo shorts.

"What's going on, guys?" Wyatt asked.

"Let me tell you what's going on," William snapped from over near the counter. "Somebody left their dead person in our wall."

Wyatt and Maggie walked toward the back of the shop, with Robert trailing nervously behind them.

Maggie got her first look at the scene, and noted that they'd cleared the counter where the cash register sat and removed the work counter that had been against the wall behind it. The wall was now missing a good portion of its sheetrock, and there was a narrow, ragged hole in the brick beneath. Through the hole, Maggie and Wyatt could see the source of William's agitation.

"Huh," Maggie said after a moment. She set her red crime scene case down on the counter.

Wyatt's upper lip tried to crawl up his nose, to block the smell of mold and age and something underlying them, something that had once smelled much worse.

"Have you touched it or moved it or anything?' Maggie asked, staring at the remains.

"Well, I touched up his hair a little," William said.

"Don't be rude," Robert said.

"I'm not being rude, I'm being upset." William snapped. "When this gets out, the only business we'll have is from the freaks and the corpse whisperers, and we'll be eating ramen in the dark because we can't afford groceries and electric."

Wyatt took a digital camera out of Maggie's tool kit as she pulled on a pair of gloves.

"It's not that bad, guys," Wyatt said. "Remember last year, when they found that dead clown in the walk-in cooler at The Driftwood? No big deal. A few weeks later everything was back to normal."

"That was different. Everybody hates clowns," William said. "This is a regular person."

Maggie yanked her long, dark brown hair into a bun, then slipped a pair of light blue plastic booties over her shoes. As Wyatt grabbed some booties of his own, she walked around the counter to get a better look at the regular person in question.

Clearly it was a man and, equally clearly, he'd been dead for some time. Only a few thin tufts of hair remained, longish strands that started out some kind of strawberry-blond color, then went gray for several inches at the roots. The eyes were gone, for all intents and purposes, and the skin was dry and papery, like that of perfectly roasted chicken.

Maggie studied the body as she heard Wyatt shuffle around the counter. She stepped a little to the side as he started clicking away.

"What do you think, Lt. Redmond?" she heard Robert ask quietly behind her.

After a moment, Maggie answered over her shoulder. "Well, you're right. He's definitely dead."

"This we parsed out on our own," William said snippily. "We've watched every single episode of *Bones*." He looked to Robert for confirmation. "Have we not?"

"Well, until Season Six. Then there was the thing."

"Oh, yes. The Mr. Nigel Murray thing. We cut our ties."

Robert snapped his fingers. "Like that."

Maggie looked over at Wyatt to see if he had a straight face. Admirably, he did. He was focused on taking pictures of the body. She took a step closer to the wall and peered at the face. Up close, the smell was enough to elicit a gentle cough, but at this point in the body's tenure, the odor could easily be mistaken for black mold. This was aided by the fact that there *was* black mold in the wall from the recent flooding.

She turned to look at William and Robert. "The wall was here when you bought the place?"

"Yes," Robert answered.

"When was that?"

"1993," William said.

"Ninety-two," Robert countered. "Remember? Hurricane Andrew hit like three weeks after we moved up here."

"1992," William said to Maggie.

Maggie looked over at Wyatt. "So, this man has been here for at least twenty-three years."

"We've had wine and cheese parties in here for crying out loud," William said.

Maggie looked back at the body as Wyatt snapped some more pictures. This type of body was way beyond her expertise. As one of two full-time investigators for the Sheriff's Office, she'd been extensively trained in crime scene investigation and gotten a good deal of training and experience in examining remains, but she'd never had to examine a body that had been dead for more than a year.

She pulled out her cell phone and dialed Larry Davenport, the county medical examiner.

"Who are you calling?" she heard William ask.

She looked over her shoulder at him. "The medical examiner."

"We're doomed," he said.

"Done for," Robert added.

"You're not doomed," Maggie said. "And I don't have any choice. This is the procedure."

"Can't you guys take him wherever he needs to go?"

"What, in the back of my Jeep?" Maggie turned back around as Larry answered the phone. "Larry, it's Maggie Redmond."

"Good evening, Maggie," Larry replied. "How may I help you?"

"We have a dead body at The Blooming Idiot," Maggie answered.

"Goodness. It's neither William nor Robert, I hope."

"No, this has been here for a while. They found it in one of the walls."

Larry was quiet for a moment. "Well, that's curious. Let me call a crew and I'll be there in a few moments."

"Do me a favor and come through the alley, okay?"

"We can do that."

Maggie said goodbye and disconnected the call. When she looked over her shoulder, William and Robert were looking at her like she'd just kicked their new kitten.

"Guys. This is the way we have to do things. I can't just sneak him out of here for you. I can't touch him at all until Larry signs off." Maggie sighed. "It's not like everybody won't know about it by morning anyway. The newspaper's a block away."

"That ferret-faced Woody Dumont," William said, meaning the newspaper's perpetually agitated editor. "He's going to think it's his birthday. He loathes us."

Wyatt spoke into his own phone. "Hey, Carol. I need a cruiser over here at The Blooming Idiot to secure a crime scene. Just one cruiser, and tell them to skip the lights and sirens. Time is not of the essence."

He hung up and looked over at the flustered florists. "Why don't you guys go home? It'll be easier if you're not in the way. I can come over there and ask you some questions when we're done here."

William and Robert looked at each other, then back at Wyatt.

"How long will you be here?" Robert asked.

"I don't know. An hour, two?"

William leaned over and whispered something to Robert, who whispered something back. Then he held out his hand and Robert dug a set of keys from his pocket and handed them to him. William held them out to Wyatt.

"You'll lock up?"

"Yeah, sure," Wyatt answered as he took the keys.

"Make sure they zip him up tight in one of those bags," William said.

"They will," Wyatt answered, frowning.

"If they get any of his flotsam or jetsam on our new bamboo floor, I'll throw myself in the street," William explained firmly.

"No flotsam or jetsam," Robert repeated for clarity.

A few minutes after Wyatt scooted the men out the door, Larry Davenport arrived, tattered black medical bag in hand, and picked gingerly through the bricks to stand in front of the wall.

Larry was somewhere in his seventies and well over six feet tall, but built like a Sandhill crane. With his carefully combed tuft of white hair and his black plastic glasses, he always put Maggie in mind of a science teacher from some 1950s movie.

He pushed his glasses up the bridge of his nose and looked at the body in the wall.

"Well, well," he said after a few moments. "I thought he'd never turn up."

Maggie looked from the body to Larry. "He who?"

Larry stepped closer to the wall and tilted his head up to adjust his bifocals. "If I'm not mistaken, this is Holden Crawford."

"How can you know that? And who is Holden Crawford?' Wyatt asked.

Larry looked over his shoulder at Wyatt. "He used to own this building, back when it was part of Crawford Seafood. Back when there *was* a Crawford Seafood. He went missing some years ago. We finally presumed him dead."

"I've never heard of him," Wyatt said.

"Oh, this was well before your time," Larry said. Wyatt had been hired to sheriff Franklin County only ten years prior. "Decades."

"Which decade?" Maggie asked. She didn't recall the name, either.

"The seventies," Larry said. "I'm not sure which one. Seventy-five, seventy-six, perhaps?"

"So why are you so sure this is him?' Wyatt asked.

Larry turned back around to peer at the body. "Well, aside from the fact that he's here, in this building, there's his Dickies."

"His what?"

"Dickies. His overalls. You can make them out there, through the plastic. Holden wore nothing else, except for church or a funeral."

"I see," Wyatt said.

Larry got his face within inches of the face in the wall, and looked down through his bifocals as though he were about to ask the man if he was in fact Crawford. "Yes, I believe that's who we have here. Of course, that's not official."

"It's unlikely we'll have any DNA on file for him," Maggie said.

"No, certainly not," Larry replied. "But before Victor Manning was the only dentist in town, his father Karl was. I imagine there are records somewhere. I'll request them."

"What were the circumstances of his disappearance?" Maggie asked.

"Oh, goodness, I don't remember all the details. I wasn't the medical examiner back then. I was just running my practice. I do recall, though, that the prevailing theory was he'd been killed."

Maggie stared at the body. "Since it's unlikely he bricked himself up in that wall, I'd say the prevailing theory prevails."

"We can assume that for the moment," Larry agreed.

Maggie focused on the body again for a moment, chewing at the corner of her lip.

"What bothers me is that he had to have smelled pretty bad back then," she said finally.

"Most likely. Most of what we're smelling right now is black mold." Larry agreed. "But back then, the wall wouldn't have done a thorough job of containing the smell. He's not wrapped especially well, and fluids would have seeped through in any event. That's if he was interred shortly after death. If someone waited a while and then moved him here, he might not have been quite as...soppy, shall we say."

Wyatt finished taking pictures and sighed. "Delightful."

He pulled his phone back out and dialed. After a moment, he said, "Hey, Dwight. I need you to dig up an old missing persons case from the seventies. Holden Crawford. Just leave it on my desk and I'll take a look first thing in the morning." He hung up and looked at Maggie. "A forty-year old case is going to be an asspain. But at least there's one nice thing."

"What's that?"

"Well, since he didn't move here until the eighties some time, I'd say we finally have one case this year that doesn't involve Bennett Boudreaux."

"You don't," Larry said from where he crouched on the floor.

Maggie and Wyatt both looked over at the birdlike old man. Wyatt sighed and put his hands on his hips. "Why not?"

"I don't remember why exactly, but I do remember that most people assumed Bennett Boudreaux did something with Holden."

Maggie felt a sinking sensation in her chest as Wyatt looked over at her, his formidable eyebrows knotted together. Maggie's odd friendship with Boudreaux was the one discord between herself and Wyatt.

He curled his finger at her, and she followed him into the back hallway. Halfway to the open back door, he stopped and turned on her. "He didn't even live here yet and he's a freaking suspect!" he said, managing somehow to yell in a whisper.

"I haven't had a decent case in over a month," she whispered back. "You are not taking it away from me just because Larry says he thinks maybe Boudreaux was involved. He's got to mean Boudreaux's father. Boudreaux was still in Louisiana back then."

Maggie was only five-three and Wyatt more than a foot taller. He loomed over her, but she jerked her chin up at him defiantly as he poked a finger in her direction.

"See?" he spat out. "Asspain."

"Let's just see what the case file says before you get all worked up over Boudreaux."

"We're working it together. Regardless of what the case file says."

As the Sheriff, Wyatt oversaw all cases, but he and Maggie had the most investigative experience in the department, and they had partnered on cases together many times. It was how they'd become best friends. But Maggie took a modicum of umbrage over the fact that he was insisting on it this time, good reason notwithstanding. True, she had come to kind of like Boudreaux, but that didn't mean she'd lost all impartiality.

"Larry's remembering it wrong. He's gotta be thinking of Boudreaux's father."

"Well, I'd be delighted if one dead guy killed the other dead guy, but Larry specifically remembers that it was Bennett that was under suspicion."

"Larry came to court last week wearing one brown shoe and one black one."

Wyatt was about to respond when the paramedic truck pulled up to the back door. He looked over his shoulder at it, then looked back at Maggie. He jabbed his finger at her chest one more time, then turned and went to meet the EMTs.

CHAPTER
THREE

A little over an hour later, Wyatt locked the front door of the shop from the inside. The deputies who'd secured the scene had marked the outside of the door with yellow crime scene tape, though only a few people, including the newspaper editor Woody Dumont, had noticed the hubbub.

Maggie and Wyatt walked silently out the back door, locking it behind them, as Larry and the EMTs pulled out of the alley and headed for Weems Memorial Hospital, where Larry's small morgue was located.

Wyatt followed Maggie around the corner and to her Jeep, then they leaned on opposite sides of the Cherokee's roof and stared at each other.

"You want to come with me to take a statement from the guys?" he asked her finally.

"Yeah." She played with her keys for a moment as she looked off down the street, chewing her lip in the way she did when she was thinking.

"What's on your mind?" Wyatt asked her after a moment.

"I'm wondering how long it takes to put up a brick wall," she answered. "I mean, this was a place of business. People were around, right?"

"We would assume."

"So, somebody not only knew how to put up the wall, they also knew they could get it done without anyone seeing them do it. Or questioning it if they did see it."

"Good point."

Maggie's phone chirped at her, and she pulled it out of the back pocket of her jeans. It was her seventeen-year-old daughter, Skyler. "Hey, Sky."

"Hey. I know you and Wyatt Earp are on a date and everything, but Kyle just yakked all over the kitchen and the bathroom. I guess he's sick. What do you want me to do?"

"Does he have a fever?"

"I don't know. I haven't checked yet."

"Well, take his temperature for me." Maggie looked over at Wyatt. "I'll be home in a few minutes."

"Sorry."

"It's okay. I got called out on a case, anyway."

"The mummy at the flower shop?" Sky asked.

"How do you know about that?"

"Dude. Twitter."

Maggie sighed and disconnected the call. She looked over at Wyatt, who was frowning at her as he drummed his fingers on the roof.

"So, this was fun,' he said.

"If it makes you feel any better, I would have preferred slow dancing, too," Maggie said.

"It doesn't really, but thank you." Wyatt said. "Everything okay at home?"

"Kyle's sick."

"Well, take me back to my car and I'll go talk to the guys myself. Then I'll go home and stuff my salad back in the bag."

"Okay," Maggie said.

They looked at each other for a moment.

"I don't think we've quite got the hang of dating," Wyatt said finally.

⚓ ⚓ ⚓

Maggie lived several miles north of town, at the end of a dirt road that was itself at the end of Bluff Road. Her home was a cypress stilt house on five wooded acres on the river. Her father's father had built it back in the 1950s, and her parents had given it to her when she and her late ex-husband had married.

Maggie drove past the chicken yard and the raised bed garden, and parked in the gravel area in front of the house. As she climbed out, her Catahoula Parish Leopard Hound, Coco, raced gravity down the deck stairs, managing not to crash in a heap at the bottom.

Maggie knelt down as Coco jubilantly met her half-way to the house.

"Hey, baby, how are you?" Maggie asked as she rubbed the dog's neck. She straightened up and looked around for the other half of the property's security team, but he was nowhere to be seen.

Coco followed her up the stairs, solid new stairs Maggie and her dad had built a couple of months ago, after the original stairs were washed away during Hurricane Faye. Maggie reached the deck and stopped in front of the door. There, on the other side of the screen door, was her Ameraucana rooster, Stoopid.

He had his neck feathers fully-deployed and his wings partially so, and was sending his usual barrage of news and questions through the screen. Stoopid had been under a great deal of stress since hatching, and always had a lot to discuss when Maggie got home. None of it was intelligible, but all of it was clearly urgent.

"*Why* are you on that side of the door?" Maggie asked him. He hit her with another string of *brrps* and coughs and other assorted noises she was supposed to understand, then backed up and did a few tight circles as she opened the door and walked in.

"Relax," Maggie said to him as she walked past him and headed for the kitchen. "It wasn't the real Lon Chaney."

Coco tossed Stoopid a resentful look that was largely ignored, then dog and bird followed Maggie into the small kitchen off of the open living and dining area.

"Y'all, I've told you to stop letting Stoopid in the house," Maggie called out. She dropped her purse and cell phone onto the kitchen counter, then nearly tripped over first Coco and then Stoopid as she turned back around.

Sky came around the corner from the hallway.

"If we leave him out there, he just does his weirdness in the windows," Sky said.

"Let him," Maggie answered. "He's gotta get over the idea that there's such a thing as a house rooster."

Maggie had brought Stoopid into the house during the hurricane, and he'd remained inside for a couple of days while Maggie had recuperated at the hospital from related injuries. In the two months since, he had insisted he was an indoor pet.

Maggie had learned that trying to catch him and chuck him out the door was more aggravation than she needed. Stoopid would run around the kitchen island, or back and forth over its bottom shelf, until she was sorely tempted to drop-kick him into the crock pot.

Instead, she opened the fridge, an act Stoopid found endlessly exciting, and grabbed a handful of apple peels from the scrap bowl. Stoopid tapped along after her as she went to the front door, swung open the screen door, and tossed the peels onto the deck.

He flapped out after his snack, and Maggie let the door slap shut. "Go tend to your women while you're out there," she said, and turned back to Sky.

"Is Kyle lying down?" she asked.

"Yeah."

"What was his temperature?"

"It was only 99.5. But he threw up again," Sky said. "'Course, that might have been because I told him I accidentally used a rectal thermometer."

"Sky," Maggie said, then sighed and jammed her fists onto her hips.

"Come on, it was funny."

Maggie stared at her daughter. Sky was nearly her double, with long dark hair, large green eyes, and full lips. One of the few differences was that Sky had her father's cleft chin. She was incredibly beautiful, and almost resentful of it.

"Just for that, you can go clean up the ninety-seven splats Stoopid left for you in front of the door," Maggie told her.

Sky rolled her eyes, but walked into the kitchen to grab some paper towels. Maggie headed down the hall and walked through Kyle's open bedroom door.

While Sky was nearly Maggie's doppelganger, Kyle was the image of his father. His hair was the same silky black. His big green eyes were almond-shaped like his dad's, and covered with the same ridiculously thick lashes. Three months after her ex-husband's death, the sight of her son could still take the breath from her.

Kyle was propped up on his pillows, watching something on his tablet. He looked up as Maggie walked in.

"Hey, Mom."

"Hey, buddy." Maggie sat on the side of the bed. "How are you feeling?"

"Kinda crappy," he answered. "Sorry about your dinner with Wyatt."

"No big deal. I ended up having to work anyway." Maggie leaned over and placed a hand on Kyle's cheek. He didn't feel warm. "What are you watching?"

"Just some Minecraft mod videos."

"Do you want something to drink?"

"Nah, I'm okay." He looked up at her. "It was probably just Sky's Mexican ramen noodles."

"That sounds like a good bet," Maggie said.

⚓   ⚓   ⚓

After taking a hot shower and throwing on some yoga pants and an old Boss Oyster tee shirt, Maggie poured a glass of Muscadine wine and let Coco outside for a bedtime pee. She leaned against the rail and waited as Coco diligently divided her urine between seventeen different key locations.

Boudreaux. Maggie would appreciate it if he turned out to be uninvolved in this case. Until this past summer, Maggie had barely known Bennett Boudreaux. Then she'd been called to the scene when Boudreaux's nephew Gregory had shot himself on the beach on St. George Island. Unwilling to share the secret that Gregory had raped her when she was just fifteen, Maggie had worked the case, and gotten to know and reluctantly like Boudreaux.

She'd suspected Boudreaux knew about her connection to Gregory, and her suspicion was confirmed when the leg of Gregory's best friend Sport Wilmette had turned up in a shrimp net a few weeks later. Boudreaux had, in his oblique way, let Maggie know that he'd killed Sport because Sport had stood by and watched Gregory rape her and dishonor the Boudreaux family.

At that point, Maggie had had to confess to Wyatt her connection to both Gregory and Sport. For a time, it had seemed like her silence, and her working of both cases, would finish her budding romance with Wyatt before it had really gotten started. Wyatt had taken over the case, but been at a disadvantage, unable to investigate effectively while keeping Maggie's secret. The fact that he had chosen to keep it spoke volumes

The situation was further confused, for both Maggie and Wyatt, when Boudreaux had saved her life, and probably the lives of her kids, when he'd shown up during the hurricane to find a man in the process of choking Maggie to death. Boudreaux had cut the man's throat, an act that no one in local law enforcement considered worth prosecuting.

Maggie took a long swallow of her wine and listened to the wind moving through the live oaks and pines on her property. There was just a hint of brine in the air from the creek on one side of her house and the river half a mile behind it. She closed her eyes, breathed it in deeply, and willed it to clear her head.

It was extremely unlikely, and would be painfully ironic, if Boudreaux turned out to be involved in this particular case. Maggie didn't remember when Boudreaux had moved from Louisiana to Apalachicola to take over his father's oyster business, but she knew it had been in the eighties.

She hadn't seen much of Boudreaux since the hurricane. Their shared experience during the storm had solidified something that had been building between them; some kind of mutual liking and respect, despite their conflicting positions. However, Maggie had seen very little of him since then, and had begun to think perhaps their friendship had been a temporary thing, brought on by their mutual connection to Gregory Boudreaux, and washed back out to the bay with the floodwaters from the storm.

As Coco ran up the deck stairs, accompanied by the percussion of collar, tags, and toenails, Maggie swallowed the last of her nightly wine and turned to go back inside. Regardless of whether or not Boudreaux was involved, there was nothing she could do about it tonight, except squelch the urge to call him up and ask him.

CHAPTER

FOUR

Five minutes after she'd hit the snooze button, Maggie was jarred within an inch of her life by Stoopid, who stood on the sill outside her bedroom window, screaming through the screen. She considered grabbing her Glock from the nightstand and shooting him, but the window screen was new.

Instead, she rolled over and pulled her grandmother's quilt over her head. This wouldn't have helped much anyway, but her cell phone went off a few seconds later. She groaned as she picked it up and looked at it. It was Wyatt.

"What," she said, by way of answering.

"Aren't you up yet?"

"I'm awake, but not up."

"Well, you should hurry up and come in," he said. "It was my turn to pick up the *café con leche*, and I'm tempted to drink yours."

"Don't. And what are you doing there so early?"

"Reading the Crawford file."

"Without me?" she asked.

"Yes, I was taught to read at an early age—"

"Please shut up."

"In any event—"

Just then, Stoopid let loose with another of his alerts that the day had permission to begin.

"Is there an elderly man throwing up in your bedroom?" Wyatt asked after a moment.

"Stoopid is crowing."

"No, he actually isn't," Wyatt said. "In any event, you need to come on in and see what we have here."

Maggie swung her legs over the side of the bed and stood up. "Judging by your forced cheerfulness, I'm guessing that I won't like it."

"I'm guessing you won't, either."

"Great." Maggie tossed a slipper at the window screen and Stoopid shut up mid-vomit. "Give me thirty minutes."

"Bring more coffee," Wyatt said before she hung up.

⚓ ⚓ ⚓

He wasn't at his desk when Maggie passed his office door. This turned out to be because he was at hers. She put the tray of coffees down on the desk, dropped her purse in a drawer, and sat down in the metal chair she used for company. Wyatt took off his reading glasses and set them atop a thick open file folder.

"So Holden Crawford went missing on August 14th, 1977," he said, reaching for his coffee.

Well, that explained why she'd never heard of the man; she hadn't even been born until the following year. Even in a town like Apalachicola, news went cold faster than that.

"Subsequently, some guy named Roland Fitch reported that he'd seen a man he thought was Crawford that night, in front of his oyster processing business."

"This is in front of what is now the flower shop?"

"No, but that's an interesting thing that we'll come back to," Wyatt answered. "Crawford's place was in that empty building just before you get to Boss Oyster."

Maggie took a sip of her *café con leche*. "Next door to Boudreaux's business?"

Wyatt gave her a halfhearted grin. "As it happens."

"Okay."

"Okay, so this guy Fitch lived across the street and down the block a little ways, and he said it was dark, but that he was pretty sure it was Crawford, and he was talking to another man, a man he described as short and slightly built."

"That fits Boudreaux, but it fits a lot of guys."

"It does," Wyatt said with a nod. "However, the reason Boudreaux, and it was *your* Boudreaux—"

"I don't have my own personal Boudreaux."

"Oh, but you do. Anyway, the reason Boudreaux was a suspect is that he got into a pretty public altercation with Crawford earlier that evening over at Papa Joe's."

"Wait," she said. "What was he doing here in Apalach?"

"Visiting his father, Alban."

Maggie looked up at the ceiling for a moment, thinking.

"Stop trying to do math in your head," Wyatt said. "He was twenty-two."

"Somehow, I can't imagine him being that young."

"You don't have to," Wyatt answered, rifling through the papers in front of him. "The sheriff at the time requested his record from Terrebonne Parish, Louisiana. They faxed this over."

He handed a piece of paper across the desk and Maggie took it. She'd always thought Boudreaux a handsome man, but the young man staring up at her looked like a darker-haired James Dean.

"What was in his record?"

"Not much. He got into a fight at a football game when he was in high school, broke some rich kid's nose."

"Huh." Maggie couldn't help staring at the picture. Even though it was a mug shot, and the murky, black-and-white fax did nothing to enhance it, Boudreaux was extremely magnetic.

"Can we get off of Boudreaux for a minute?" Wyatt asked. "Because I'm trying to tell you what Fitch said he saw."

"Okay."

"So, he said Crawford, or at least he was pretty sure it was Crawford, was outside his place talking to this shorter guy. He said Crawford's voice was raised, like they were arguing, but he couldn't hear what he was saying. Then this smaller guy punches him—"

"Crawford."

"—punches Crawford in the stomach." Wyatt continued. "Fitch briefly considered running down there to help him out, but then this other guy comes out Crawford's front door and rushes over to them, yelling. So Fitch scurries back inside. Said it wasn't his business, but what he meant was he didn't want to get his ass kicked."

"Did he know the other man, the taller one that came out afterwards?"

"No, too dark, too far away." Wyatt flipped a sheet of paper over. "Anyway, a couple of minutes later, Fitch heard a car and looked out his window, and Crawford's car was headed down the street, going the other way, and the men were gone."

"Okay," Maggie said. "Where was Crawford's car after he went missing?"

"Nowhere. They never found it," Wyatt answered. "They did, however, find some blood out in front of Crawford's place. Same blood type as Crawford's. The days before DNA, bless our hearts."

"How much blood?" Maggie asked.

"Not a lot."

Maggie took a drink of her coffee and stared at the edge of her desk for a moment. "So, either Crawford and these other guys took off in his car, or Crawford drove off and the other guys left on foot, or these guys took off in Crawford's car with him in it."

"These are our options," Wyatt said.

"And this was all on August 14th, the night Crawford was last seen." The date rang a bell with Maggie, niggled at her. She pushed the thought back for later.

"Yeah," Wyatt answered, then flipped a few more pages. "So, there's plenty left here for you to go through, but let me give you some other highlights. There's a notation on the log that the sheriff himself was scheduled to question Boudreaux, but there's no statement in here. However, there is a note that he was questioned, and that he had an alibi for the time Fitch thinks he saw Crawford and the other guy. Only, there's no mention of what said alibi was."

Maggie chewed at her lower lip. "Okay. Who *was* the sheriff back then?"

"Guy named Bradford Wilson."

"I knew Wilson. Sort of. He was friends with my grandparents."

"Well, he sucked at documentation." Wyatt flipped a few pages. "Anyway, he resigned in 1990 and was succeeded by my predecessor, Martin Vanick."

"He moved somewhere a long time ago, but he might be dead by now."

"No, but he probably wishes he was. Carol says he moved to Panama City Beach."

"Ew."

"Yeah. So, he's old, but he's still there. Got his number."

"Does our dead man have family? I don't know any Crawfords."

"No kids, but he had a wife who never remarried. She's in a nursing home over in Port St. Joe."

"Well, we can't talk to her until we know for sure that our body is Crawford." Maggie's chin lifted just slightly. "The whole thing about Boudreaux could be irrelevant."

"It could, but it won't be, because that's the kind of luck you have."

Maggie opted out of a retort, took a sip of her coffee instead. "So tell me the interesting thing we're going back to, about the flower shop," she said after a moment.

"Yeah, the flower shop," Wyatt said. "Crawford owned it, but it wasn't part of the seafood business. He owned two or three of those spaces. They'd been empty for years. He was having them remodeled so he could put a raw bar and some shops in there."

"They were being remodeled when he went gone?"

"Yes."

"Huh."

"That's what I said." Wyatt took a hearty swallow of his coffee. "So the building wasn't open. It was a construction site."

"Why was that even in the file?"

"When Crawford first went missing, they checked the site out to make sure he hadn't gone over there and gotten injured. But the theory was whatever happened, happened to him that night at his oyster business."

"What about this altercation between Crawford and Boudreaux?"

"In the file. Have fun." Wyatt checked the time on his cell phone. "I have to go talk to James about some robbery over in Eastpoint last night."

He stood, and Maggie followed suit. As she squeezed past Wyatt to get to her desk chair, she caught a faint whiff of his cologne and just a hint of laundry detergent. He looked down at her as they passed each other, and he was so close, Maggie couldn't help but glance through her open office door to make sure no one could see them so comfortable in each other's space.

Wyatt reflexively glanced over his shoulder, then looked back at Maggie as she sat down in her chair. "Paranoia. Nature's aphrodisiac."

Maggie opened the file back up as Wyatt headed for the door. "You remember when I was in the hospital and you said you weren't speaking to me?"

"Yes."

"I resent that you haven't made good on that yet."

"You're precious," Wyatt said as he walked out.

Maggie took a long swallow of her coffee and flipped the thick file to the beginning.

⚓   ⚓   ⚓

Two hours, one and a half coffees, and three restroom breaks later, Maggie closed the file and leaned back in her chair, the fax image of Bennett Boudreaux in her hand. She'd referred to it several times as she'd read the contents of the case file. Boudreaux was probably the most quietly charismatic man she'd ever met, and she thought so in a strictly platonic way, but the image of him as a man only five years older than her daughter was almost hypnotic. The fact that she couldn't see the brilliant aquamarine of his eyes made no difference in how piercing those eyes were.

She didn't want Boudreaux to be involved in this case. Over the summer, she had gone from a surprising and grudging respect for the man to a genuine though reluctant liking of him. However, what they'd gone through together during Hurricane Faye had borne in her a certain sense of gratitude and responsibility. Those were bad things for a law enforcement officer to feel toward a known criminal. She knew that, and while she wasn't helpless to change it, she was unwilling. The man had been seriously injured while saving the lives of herself and her kids.

Maggie felt that itching at the edges of her frontal lobe again, and she sat up, leaned on her desk, and started tapping a pen on the dented metal. After a moment, it came to her, and she almost wished it hadn't.

August 14th. The day Bennett Boudreaux had saved her life.

CHAPTER

FIVE

ennett Boudreaux lived in the heart of Apalach's historic district, a neighborhood that surprised many visitors with its combination of cracker cottages and gingerbread Victorians, brick colonials and Greek Revivals. Apalach was a lot more northern than most tourists expected it to be, a result of the southern migration of entrepreneurs eager to succeed in the cotton trade.

Boudreaux's home was a white, plantation-style home with a wraparound porch, set on an unusually large corner lot. It would have commanded more than a million dollars if it was on the market, but the house was a lot like Boudreaux; modest roots dressed in understated elegance.

Boudreaux sat at the table in the kitchen, bathed in the early morning sunlight that streamed through the original twelve-pane windows. He stirred pure cane sugar into his four-dollar per can chicory coffee, which had been served in a forty-dollar Wedgewood cup, then took his first sip of the day.

At the cypress island in the middle of the kitchen, his cook and housekeeper, Amelia, stood over a cast iron skillet in which gently sizzled one perfectly round over-medium egg. One slice of maple bacon sat on a small plate next to the stove. Amelia was tall and large-boned, and her tea-colored Creole skin made it difficult to judge her age, though Boudreaux knew her to be sixty-three; just one year older than he was himself.

Amelia had worked for Boudreaux for decades. Her mother, Miss Evangeline, had been his father's housekeeper and nanny, and the only mother-figure Boudreaux had known. Boudreaux's father had moved to Apalach in the late sixties, when Boudreaux was still an adolescent. He'd left Boudreaux with Miss Evangeline, then fired her when Boudreaux had gone off to Tulane.

As soon as Boudreaux had started becoming successful at his own seafood business, he'd hired them both back, and when his father died in 1982, he'd taken over his father's business and brought the two women with him. He'd suggested many times over the last few years that Amelia might want to join her mother in retiring, but Amelia had refused rather indignantly. It was unspoken, but understood, that she and her mother would always have their cottage in the back yard, but Amelia thought there should only be 'one useless color woman to the house.'

Boudreaux opened up the newspaper and saw that the lead story, accompanied by a picture larger than his head, was about something going on at the florist downtown. The photograph showed a paramedic truck pulling out of the alley behind the shop.

Boudreaux scanned the first couple of paragraphs, then laid the paper back down on the table for a moment and slowly took a sip of his coffee. He let the slightly bitter liquid slide down his throat, then took a deep breath and let it out silently.

Maggie was handling this case. Of course she was. It was God's continuing reminder that his past was always part of his present. He wondered if his estimable influence with the city and county was enough to talk them into getting a third investigator on at the Sheriff's Office. They only had the two, and he would have appreciated it if Maggie would stop pulling cases that involved him.

He had just picked the paper back up when the back door opened and Miss Evangeline toddled through it, tailgating an aluminum walker fitted with bright green tennis balls.

His former nanny was close to one hundred years old, and her skin had the appearance of a papyrus on which someone had long ago spilled a cup of rich coffee. She stood less than five feet tall and weighed less than a sturdy fourth-grader, but she managed to be imposing nonetheless. She barked rather than spoke, and her sharp eyes, magnified behind comically thick glasses, could pin a person to a wall.

Boudreaux set the paper aside once more and rose from his seat. He walked around the table and pulled out Miss Evangeline's chair as she scooted her walker along the hardwood floor.

"Mornin', Mama," Amelia said. She slid the egg onto a small plate and pulled a slice of bread from the toaster.

"Mornin', baby," Miss Evangeline answered, her voice like footsteps on autumn leaves.

"Good morning, Miss Evangeline," Boudreaux said.

"Ain't gon' take your word," she answered.

Boudreaux kissed her on the cheek once she reached him, held her chair for her as she delicately maneuvered her person onto it. Then he easily slid her chair in and walked back to his own seat.

Amelia brought the plate and a cup of tea to the table and set them in front of her mother, then went back to the island to clean up. Miss Evangeline carefully took a sip of her tea, then proceeded to painstakingly cut her egg into fractions. She took one tiny bite and carefully chewed it before swallowing.

"Amelia, I need you go back the store and get me some new underwears," she said as she began to scrape some butter onto her toast.

"I just got you some the other day," Amelia said.

"Ain't no good. They too big," Miss Evangeline replied. "I fell right out them underwears yesterday."

Boudreaux tried not to smile as he poured another cup of coffee.

"That's 'cause you losin' too much weight, you," Amelia said. "I almost can't get you none smaller."

"I ain't lose nothin', me. You got the wrong size."

"I got the right size, Mama."

Boudreaux couldn't keep the corners of his mouth from turning up just a bit, so he hid behind a sip of coffee before he spoke. "Perhaps Amelia could get you some underthings from the girls' department," he said smoothly. "Something cheerful, like Cinderella or Hello Kitty."

Amelia groaned from the kitchen sink. Miss Evangeline stopped buttering her well-buttered toast and peered across the table at Boudreaux. He pretended not to notice as he set his cup back down on its saucer.

"What you say?" Miss Evangeline snapped.

"I said something from the girl's department might fit you more snugly. And start your day off with a smile."

"Chil'ren underwears," she said flatly.

Boudreaux gave her the slightest of shrugs as he picked his paper back up. Miss Evangeline put down her toast and sucked at a bit of egg on her upper denture before speaking.

"You woke up the mouthy side your bed, then," she said.

"Not at all," Boudreaux said smoothly. "I'm just trying to be helpful."

"Help me some more, Mr. Benny. I help you out that chair by your nose hairs, me."

Boudreaux turned to the third page of the paper, where the story continued, and scanned it quickly. The idiot editor, Dumont, had tried to sound anecdotal rather than speculative when he mentioned in the last paragraph that the building had once been owned by Holden Crawford, who had disappeared almost forty years prior.

The implication was clear, but pointless. Of course the "unidentified remains" would be Holden Crawford.

"Who go the ambulance in the paper?" Miss Evangeline barked across the table.

"Unidentified remains from inside a wall in the flower shop," Boudreaux answered distractedly.

"Who remain?"

"Somebody who died a long time ago."

"Why they find him now, then?"

"I guess he was just waiting for precisely the worst moment to turn up," Boudreaux said.

Miss Evangeline poked her Coke bottle glasses back toward her plate and took another bite of egg. "Dead folk don't ha' no regard, no. Do what they please."

"Yes."

Boudreaux had finished the article, such as it was, but he continued to stare at the print as he got caught up in his own thoughts. Of any case that Maggie could have gotten, Boudreaux would have asked that it not be this one.

"Even so," he heard Miss Evangeline say. "You put a dead body in the wall, he s'posed to stay put. Ain't no call to be runnin' round bein' dead everyplace, scarin' folk."

Boudreaux lowered the paper and looked across the table, his brows pressing together above his startling blue eyes.

"Have you taken your medication?"

⚓   ⚓   ⚓

Early in the afternoon, Maggie's cell phone rang and she picked it up off of her desk.

"Good afternoon, Maggie. It's Larry."

Maggie swung away from her monitor. "Hey, Larry. What's up?"

"We've had a spot of good luck," Larry answered. "Victor Manning has his father's patient files going all the way back to the sixties. I have Holden Crawford's dental x-rays on my desk, and Holden Crawford himself on my autopsy table."

"How fortunate," Maggie said quietly.

"Indeed."

"I don't suppose you have a cause of death yet?"

"No, not as yet, but I should have something to share with you by tomorrow."

"Okay, thank you."

Maggie hung up, then heaved a sigh. Everything would have been much simpler if it had turned out to be someone else.

She slid her cell phone into the back pocket of her jeans, then grabbed her purse and headed down the hall. She stopped in Wyatt's doorway. Wyatt was peering at his own monitor, leaning into it despite his reading glasses.

"Hey," Maggie said.

"Hey."

"We have a positive ID on the body. It's Crawford."

"You don't say," Wyatt said, taking his glasses off. "I have news, too. Guess who the flower shop guys bought their flower shop from?"

Maggie's chest suddenly felt weighted. "Who?"

"Your personal Boudreaux." Wyatt picked his Sheriff's Office ball cap up from his desk and slapped it onto his head. "Isn't that entertaining?"

Maggie sighed and looked away from Wyatt for a moment, then looked back at him. "So do you want to go with me to talk to Mrs. Crawford or what?"

"Why, yes." Wyatt unfolded himself from his chair, his endless legs almost as long as Maggie's entire body, and walked around the desk. "I'll need to stop for a Mountain Dew."

CHAPTER

SIX

ort St. Joe was a quaint little coastal town not too unlike Apalachicola, and about thirty minutes out Hwy 98. The Sunset Bay community, an assisted living and rehab facility, was just outside town. Maggie was impressed with its upper-middle class suburban feel. It looked more like an upscale gated neighborhood than it did a place old people went when they had nowhere else to go.

Wyatt whistled softly as Maggie followed the long driveway through the well-manicured grounds. "I'd say Mrs. Crawford must be pretty well off," he said.

"Looks that way," Maggie replied.

They passed a few single-story Spanish style buildings that could have been condos or vacation rentals anywhere along the coast. Here and there, elderly people tottered around their patios and flower beds, some with walkers, others in wheelchairs, and a very few without any manmade assistance. There were also several staff members, all wearing yellow polo shirts under their lab coats and sweaters.

The driveway ended in a small parking area in front of a three-story building with a fancy portico and mahogany double doors. Maggie parked and she and Wyatt walked inside to find themselves in what could have been the lobby of a nice hotel. Wyatt led the way over to a blonde, middle-aged receptionist seated behind a glassy teak desk.

"Good afternoon," she said. "May I help you?"

"Hi. Sheriff Hamilton and Lt. Redmond to see Beth Crawford. We phoned a little while ago."

"Oh, yes. If you'll wait here for just a moment, I'll have someone take you to her. She's in the Magnolia building."

"Thank you," Wyatt said.

She picked up her desk phone, and Wyatt and Maggie wandered away, looking around at the expensive looking upholstered furniture and original oils of Panhandle scenery.

"If I ever need long term care, I'd appreciate it if you made sure I ended up here," Wyatt said.

"Please. You're gonna drop dead of a heart attack with a thirty-two ounce Mountain Dew in your hand."

"You don't have to get all sentimental about it," he answered. "I'm just saying, if I get really grouchy and incontinent, this is where I want you to put me."

Maggie almost asked him why he thought it would be her task, but she was afraid he might tell her. Instead, she pretended she'd just noticed the painting of a seagull on the wall next to her.

"Officers?"

Maggie and Wyatt turned to see a young, dark-haired woman in a navy polo shirt and scrub pants.

"I'll take you over to visit Mrs. Crawford," she said. "It's just a short walk if you want to follow me."

"Thank you," Wyatt said, and opened the mahogany door for the two women, then followed them outside.

"Are you Mrs. Crawford's nurse?" Maggie asked as they walked along a brick-paved path.

"Oh, no. I work in the main building, with the more medically-needy residents. I just happen to be handy."

"So Mrs. Crawford doesn't need a nurse?" Wyatt asked.

"All of our residents have some level of medical assistance. Mrs. Crawford is in the Magnolia building, in that section up there that we call The Residences." She pointed up ahead to the cluster of one-story buildings they'd passed coming in. "Those are for residents who just need a nursing assistant and on-call medical. Each building has six apartments and one twenty-four hour CNA. One of the registered nurses visits twice daily to administer any medications and take vitals."

"So she's in good health?"

"Physically, yes, pretty good. I know she has some dementia."

"Will she be able to understand us well? Answer questions?" Wyatt asked.

"I really don't know that much about her condition," the woman answered. "But you can talk to her caregiver. I think Molly Vinson is on duty this afternoon."

They turned off the path at the second small building, and the young woman opened the front door and beckoned them in. Maggie and Wyatt walked into a hub-like room, off of which were several doors.

"Each residence has its own patio, so the residents can enjoy the outdoors, but as you can see, help is always right at hand."

A woman about Maggie's age, with red hair gathered in a loose bun, came out of one of the doors to the left and smiled at their little group in general.

"Hey, Molly. These are the officers that have come to talk to Mrs. Crawford."

The woman held her hand out to both Maggie and Wyatt in turn. "Hi, I'm Molly Vinson. I'm one of Mrs. Crawford's assistants."

"Hi," Maggie said. "Lt. Redmond."

"Sheriff Hamilton," Wyatt said as he shook the woman's hand.

"I'll leave you to your visit," the first woman said as she headed out the door.

Molly Vinson frowned at the two of them. "So is something wrong?"

"Actually, yes,' Wyatt answered. "Mrs. Crawford's husband went missing years ago. We just recovered his remains. We need to notify her."

"Oh, my gosh," the woman said.

"I imagine she assumed him dead a long time ago," Maggie said. "But is she up to this kind of news?"

"Well, is anyone?" The woman blinked few times. "But, she's pretty lucid most of the time, and she's not really a frail woman. Emotionally, I mean. She should be fine, but I'd like to go in with you."

"That's fine," Wyatt said.

"She's in Unit 5," the woman said, and led them to one of the doors at the back of the hub. She knocked lightly, and after a moment, they heard a woman's voice tell her to come in. Molly opened the door, and preceded Maggie and Wyatt into the small apartment.

The room was the size of a smallish suite at a decent hotel, with a kitchenette, sans stove, to the right and a spacious living area that ended with a sliding door to a back patio. To the left was a door that opened into a bedroom.

Beth Crawford sat at a small table near the open sliding door, a book and a cup of tea beside her. Maggie was surprised at her appearance. She'd expected a white bun and frilly robe, but this woman was nothing like the delicate little old lady that Maggie had assumed she'd be.

She was obviously fairly tall, at least five-six or seven, and she sat up straight in her chair. She was thin in the way that formerly athletic women tend to be when they get old, and her hair was a wavy ash blonde, though artificially so. The most jarring thing about her appearance was her make-up. She appeared to be wearing self-tanner, a good deal of it, and her face was thickly coated with makeup. It wasn't badly done, just done to excess for a woman in her seventies.

She looked uncertain for a moment, then smiled politely at Maggie and Wyatt. "Hello," she said in a surprisingly soft voice, and it sounded like a question.

"Mrs. Crawford, these folks are from the Franklin County Sheriff's Office and they need to speak with you."

"Hello, ma'am," Wyatt said, holding out a hand. "I'm Sheriff Hamilton, and this is Lt. Redmond."

Mrs. Crawford took and released his hand, gave Maggie a glance, then looked back up at Wyatt. "Won't you sit down?"

Wyatt and Maggie both took seats at the small round table. Molly remained standing, though she moved to stand beside her patient.

"Mrs. Crawford, I'm very sorry, but I'm afraid we have some unpleasant news," Wyatt said gently. He paused a moment, but the older woman didn't speak, just looked at him expectantly. "I'm afraid we recovered your husband's remains yesterday evening. He's been positively identified by the medical examiner."

The woman stared at him a moment, then looked over at Maggie. "Holden?"

"Yes, ma'am," Maggie answered. "We're very sorry for your loss."

The woman looked out the sliding door for a moment, seeming to focus on the cardinal that was bouncing from branch to branch in a coral hibiscus near the tiny patio. As Maggie watched, she blinked a few times, but there were no tears. Finally, she sighed softly and looked back at the two of them.

"Well, my loss took place a long time ago, didn't it?" she asked them softly. "I've known he was dead for years. Even so..." she drifted off, stared at the table a moment before looking back up at Wyatt. "Where was he?"

Wyatt took a moment to answer, his voice soothing and quiet. "He was found in the flower shop downtown, on Commerce Street."

The woman's brows pulled together and they could see her thinking. "The flower shop?"

"On Commerce Street. It's in the building your husband used to own."

Mrs. Crawford's lips pursed at that, and after a moment she nodded. "I see. But I don't understand."

"Ma'am, someone had placed his body behind a brick wall in what is now the flower shop," Wyatt said. "Someone hid his body."

They watched her think about that for a moment, as Molly placed a hand on her shoulder, a hand she didn't seem to notice.

"Well. I know it was always assumed that someone had hurt Holden, but to tell you the truth, I never really put much stock in that."

"Why not?" Wyatt asked.

"Oh, well, you know Holden," she said, though they didn't. "Everyone liked him."

She looked over at Maggie, and the light in her eyes seemed to flicker, like an overloaded circuit box. "Are you new here?" she asked Maggie.

"No, Mrs. Crawford," Maggie answered. "I'm Lt. Redmond. I work with Sheriff Hamilton," she said, gesturing at Wyatt.

"Yes, right." Mrs. Crawford looked up at Molly. "Is my tea ready yet, honey?"

"You have your tea there," the woman answered.

Mrs. Crawford frowned down at her cup. "Oh, this is cold. It's from yesterday, I think. Could you make me another cup?"

The younger woman picked up the cup, and Maggie watched her take it over to the little kitchen area. There was one of those insulated electric carafes there, and Molly dumped the contents of the cup and poured fresh tea into it.

Maggie heard Wyatt say something, and she turned back to the conversation.

"No, I don't know of anyone who had problems with him, really," Mrs. Crawford was saying.

"What about the Boudreauxes?"

The woman faltered for a moment. "Who?"

"Bennett Boudreaux and his father, Alban. Alban owned Sea-Fair."

"Oh, yes. From Louisiana." She nodded at Molly as the younger woman set the new cup of tea in front of her. "They were competitors, of course. But not the only ones."

"Your husband's case file says that Bennett Boudreaux got into a problem with your husband at Papa Joe's the night Holden disappeared," Wyatt said.

Mrs. Crawford tugged at an earlobe for a moment. For some reason, it seemed to Maggie like the gesture of a much younger woman.

"Yes, I remember something about that. I can't say I remember what it was about. I wasn't there with Holden."

"According to witnesses, they had some pretty unpleasant words," Maggie said. "Something about problems between Alban Boudreaux and your husband. Business problems."

"Oh. Well, you know, Mr. Boudreaux wanted to buy that lot next to Crawford Seafood. We owned it. I think Mr. Boudreaux wanted to expand. But Holden thought he might do the same thing sooner or later, so he didn't want to sell."

"That's it?" Wyatt asked. "That's all that was going on between them?"

"I think they had quite a few arguments about it."

"Mrs. Crawford," Maggie spoke up. "Bennett Boudreaux sold that building to the men that own it now. Did he buy it from you or from someone else?"

"Oh. I sold it to him, eventually." She took a sip of her tea. "I hung onto it for quite a while. I didn't have much choice, really, until I could legally do something with Holden's business. That was a real mess, you know, with us not knowing whether he was alive or dead. Poor Holden."

"How do you mean?" Wyatt asked gently.

"Well, we eventually had to have him declared dead you know. We all knew he had to be, but there were legal issues." She rubbed at a bright peach stain on the side of her cup. "For a while there, it was hard financially. While we waited for Holden to come back. The business was a mess, until we finally promoted one of the employees to run it for me."

"What about the other building?" Maggie asked. "The one where he was found? What was going on with it during that time?"

Mrs. Crawford needed a minute to think about that before she spoke. "The new building. Yes, well, everything stopped there. They needed money to keep renovating and I didn't have access to the money right away. It was a couple of years before they got back to work on it."

"So it was just closed up?" Wyatt asked.

"Yes. For a long time."

"Who had access to it then?"

"Oh, just me. I went over there now and then to pop in and see my husband."

"I'm sorry?" Wyatt said.

"You know, when he was working over there, seeing how things were progressing. He was so excited about that place."

"No, Mrs. Crawford," Maggie said. "We mean after your husband disappeared. Who had access to that building?"

"Yes, I know. No, nobody." She frowned at her cup. "Once they finished it, I used it for storage, for my antique business. But I'm the only one who ever went over there."

"When did Boudreaux buy the place?" Wyatt asked.

"Let me think," the woman said, her carefully-penciled brows coming together. "It was years later. I sold him the lot, too. It was right between his place and ours, you know. So, I guess the Boudreauxs got it after all."

"Do you remember when that was?" Maggie asked.

"Hm. Well, it was not too long after Mr. Boudreaux died. He had a stroke, you know. His son moved here and took over. Bennett Boudreaux did. I sold him some boats and the lot and the building downtown. I needed the money."

She rubbed at the lipstick stain on her cup again. "Oh, this lipstick," she said. "I have to order most things online now, you know, because I don't drive much. I order my cosmetics from Ulta, but it's so hard to know if something's good until you get it."

She looked up at Maggie. "What brand do you like? Oh, you don't wear lipstick."

Maggie almost felt like it was a gentle dig. "I'm more of a lip balm girl," she said.

"So, did you know Bennett Boudreaux well?" Wyatt asked.

"No, not really. Wow, he was a real looker, though," she said, smiling. "All the women went for him, though he didn't really seem all that excited about that."

Maggie watched the woman as her face seemed to undergo some sort of subtle shifting. Her smile was bigger, more gregarious, her eyes grew larger as she looked at Wyatt.

"I bet they think you're a real catch. Of course, a lot of people thought that about me, too," she said to him, and actually winked.

Wyatt smiled back, his polite smile. Maggie wondered if the woman suddenly thought she was in her thirties again. Her facial expressions and speech had become almost flirtatious. Maggie wasn't sure if it was creepy or just sad.

Wyatt stood and gently pushed his chair back in. Maggie stood with him, though she wasn't sure she'd finished asking questions.

"Mrs. Crawford, I appreciate you speaking with us," Wyatt said as the woman smiled up at him. "Again, we're very sorry for your loss. Someone will be in touch with you about making arrangements for your husband."

"Poor Holden," she said. "He really was the nicest guy."

Molly had picked up a bottle of pills, and was shaking one into her hand.

"We can see ourselves out," Wyatt told her.

A few minutes later, Maggie and Wyatt walked gratefully back into the present day sunshine, and started walking back toward the parking lot.

"I changed my mind," Wyatt said. "I don't want you to put me here. If I start losing it, just drown me in the bathtub."

"Okay," Maggie said.

"It doesn't matter how pretty the landscaping is," he said. "Losing your mind is damn ugly."

"Yes."

They walked in silence for a few moments before Maggie spoke again.

"You should know that Boudreaux once told me he would never kill for money," she said.

"Maybe it was something else."

"Maybe it wasn't Boudreaux," she said a little defensively.

"I'm keeping an open mind," he said back. "You should, too."

"I will."

When they reached the Jeep, Maggie unlocked her door and looked across the roof to ask Wyatt if he wanted to stop for lunch. He was staring off across the parking lot. Maggie looked, and saw a tall, slim man in black trousers and a white button down shirt walking toward the front doors.

"What?" Maggie asked.

"Is that Evan Caldwell?"

"Who?"

"Hey, Evan?" Wyatt called. "Evan!"

The man looked over his shoulder, then stopped. He had almost jet black hair, and when he took off his sunglasses, Maggie thought he looked familiar.

The man started walking toward them, and Maggie left her door open and followed Wyatt as he met the man halfway.

"Hey, Wyatt," the man said, his voice both rough and smooth at the same time, like good bourbon.

Wyatt held out a hand, and Caldwell took it and gave it a firm shake.

"How are you, man?" Wyatt asked him.

Caldwell nodded as an answer, and glanced over at Maggie. Wyatt looked at her, too.

"Maggie, you remember Evan Caldwell? He helped me with the Joey Francis case my first year here."

Maggie remembered him then. The missing persons expert from somewhere on the other side of the state. Wyatt had worked with him a few times back when he'd been the sheriff in Cocoa Beach.

"Yes, how are you?" she asked, holding out her hand. When he took it, his long fingers wrapped around it firmly but without commitment.

"Lieutenant," he said.

"It's good to see you," Wyatt said. "You still in Vero?"

"No. No, I moved to Port St. Joe a few months ago," Evan answered.

"No kidding. You're not retired are you?" Evan was only in his early forties, Wyatt knew.

"Somewhat," Evan answered. "I'm consulting these days."

"I'll keep that in mind," Wyatt said. "You here on a case?"

"No." Evan scratched at a narrow scar that ran from one corner of his full mouth down to his chin. "No, I'm here visiting my wife."

"Your wife. Hannah, right?"

"Yeah. She, uh, she had an accident a little while back," Evan said, looking just past Wyatt's shoulder. "There was some neurological damage. I had her moved here."

Wyatt was quiet for a moment, his eyes going warm and serious.

"Geez, man. I'm sorry."

Evan nodded, then looked back at Wyatt finally. "Thank you. This is supposed to be the best facility in the state."

Wyatt nodded. "It seems like a decent place."

The men seemed to run out of things to comfortably say, and everyone looked at the ground for a moment.

"You two working a case?" Evan finally asked.

"Yeah, we are," Wyatt answered almost gratefully. "You know Beth Crawford? Lives in that one over there?"

"No. Hannah's in the main building here. I really don't know anyone."

"Ah. Well, her husband went missing back in the seventies. We just found his body."

"Natural?"

"No. Found him in somebody's wall."

"Probably rules that out," Caldwell said quietly.

"We're thinking," Wyatt agreed.

Caldwell nodded, then looked over his shoulder at the front door. "I should get inside. Good luck with the case."

Wyatt shook the man's hand. "It was good to see you, Evan. I hope your wife's better soon."

Evan nodded noncommittally then raised a hand at Maggie. "You two take care."

They watched him walk away, then they headed back to the Jeep. Wyatt didn't speak until they were both buckled in.

"She's only like forty years old, you know," he said to the windshield.

Maggie put the key in the ignition, but she didn't start the car. She sat and watched Wyatt as he frowned out at nothing.

"I only met her a few times, but she was a neat lady. Beautiful."

Maggie waited, as Wyatt took his cap off, ran a hand through his hair, then slapped the hat back down on his head.

"Let's get out of here," he said. "I hate this place."

So, you think she gets it that he's actually dead?" Wyatt said as he unnecessarily salted his fries.

"I think she's known it for a long time." Maggie stuck her straw into her sweet tea and crumpled up the wrapper. "Whether she'll always know that is another thing."

"What did you think of her?" Wyatt took a bite of his grouper sandwich, then immediately opened his mouth back up. "Hot," he sort of said.

"Of course it's hot. Why don't you wait three seconds?"

"Ah...gah," he said, trying to get cooling air into his mouth and chew at the same time.

Maggie rolled her eyes and waited while he gingerly chewed and swallowed. Once he had, he shrugged sheepishly. "Hot grouper."

Maggie sighed and thought about her words for a moment, staring out the window at the little marina where they'd stopped. "I think she's one of those veneer women."

"What does that mean exactly?" He stared at the sandwich in his hand, as though gauging its temperature.

"One of those women who focus on appearing to be what they want other people to think they are."

"Huh." Wyatt started to take another bite, then aborted before he actually broke a piece off. "Hot."

"Do you need me to blow on it for you?" Maggie asked sarcastically.

"I'm starving," he said. He took the top off of the sandwich and set it aside. "So do you think she was giving us some kind of crap?"

Maggie shrugged. "No, I just think that's who she is. Kind of like some of the soccer moms, you know, always presenting this perfect image."

"You're a soccer mom," he said.

"I'm a softball and baseball mom."

"Which differs in what way?"

"It's just a term."

"You don't like her."

Maggie thought about that for a moment. "I don't know her."

"Was it the lipstick thing?" Wyatt waved ineffectually over his sandwich, then looked up at her. "I happen to like your lip balm."

Maggie managed not to smile, busied herself with her grouper chowder.

"So, after lunch we'll put go on over and talk to our former sheriff." Wyatt said. "Since we're halfway to PCB anyway."

"Okay."

"I'd also like to hear what he says about all this before we hear your friend's side of the story."

"He's not my friend."

"No? What is he then?"

She was about to answer when her cell phone buzzed in her back pocket. She pulled it out and looked. She recognized the number from the night before.

"Ugh," Maggie said before connecting the call. "Hello, William."

"Sheriff, it's William the florist," William explained unnecessarily. "When will you people be done with our shop?"

"The crime scene techs are going back there today, if they haven't already," she answered.

"They haven't been here yet. The crime scene tape is still on the door, and passerby are looking askance at me."

"I'm sorry about that."

"Robert was sct upon at Piggly-Wiggly this morning by three different people who were relieved he was okay," he said. "Like it couldn't have been *me* in the wall."

"They should be finished sometime today," Maggie said. "I'll be stopping by there later on, too."

"I really need to get that wall out of there," he said. Maggie heard him take a long drag on a cigarette and blow it out. "I'm besieged by heebies and also jeebies."

"I understand. I'm sorry you're dealing with this. We'll get things back to normal as quickly as possible, okay?"

She heard him heave a sigh that should have snapped at least one rib.

"Please do," he said, then disconnected.

Maggie set the phone down on the table and looked at Wyatt. He tried not to smile as he chewed and swallowed.

"I don't think he's as fond of you as he used to be," he said.

⚓ ⚓ ⚓

Bradford Wilson, former Sheriff of Franklin County, was now the proud owner of one of the three-thousand T-shirt shops on the strip in Panama City Beach.

The town was fairly quiet at that time of the year, and Maggie had no trouble finding a place to park in the small lot beside the shop. They walked through the open door, made their way through racks of shirts, hats and flip-flops, and ended up at a wooden counter in back.

The man standing behind the counter reading a fishing magazine was almost as tall as Wyatt, but quite a bit heavier and many years older. His hair and beard were mostly gray, and he didn't seem anxious to keep up with the maintenance of either one.

He looked up as Maggie and Wyatt approached, noting their navy blue polo shirts with the Sheriff's Office insignia. "Well, hello there," he said in a deep voice. "What's Franklin's finest doing in PCB?"

"Mr. Wilson?" Wyatt asked.

The man held out a huge hand. "That's me. And you would be Sheriff Hamilton, correct? Seen you in the paper a few times."

"Yes, I am," Wyatt answered, shaking the man's hand. "This is Lt. Redmond."

"Lieutenant." He started to look away, then smiled at Maggie. "Wait a minute. Maggie Redmond?"

"Yes," she answered.

He smiled broadly. "I see you followed in your grandfather's footsteps.

"Yes, I guess so." Maggie's maternal grandfather had been with the Apalach PD for thirty years.

"He was like a mentor to me,' Wilson said.

"Me, too," Maggie said.

"I was sorry to read about your Grandma passing. She was a great lady."

"Thank you. She was."

"How's your mother?"

"She's doing well, thank you. My dad's semi-retired now, so she's happily busy making him remodel their house."

His eyes flickered for a second, as though he was trying to recall her father's name. "Gray," he said finally.

"Yes."

He smiled again, but it was more polite than warm. "We're all getting old." He looked over at Wyatt. "So what brings you here?"

"Holden Crawford. He disappeared in '77," Wyatt answered. "Do you remember the case?"

Wilson looked from Wyatt to Maggie and back again. "Now that was a long time ago. But, yes, I remember."

"We found his remains yesterday."

It took a minute for Wilson to respond, though his face was blank. "Where?"

"He was bricked up in a wall. A building down on Commerce Street," Wyatt answered.

The man nodded slowly, then looked around him. "Let's grab some chairs, huh?"

He indicated they should come behind the counter, then pulled out a couple of metal folding chairs. He sat down on a torn leather bar stool and waited while Wyatt and Maggie got seated.

"Do you remember the case?" Maggie asked.

He frowned at her. "Sure. Somewhat."

"When you guys checked those buildings he was remodeling, do you remember if there was a brick wall in the flower shop?" Wyatt asked.

"I don't know of a flower shop over there."

"It's in the unit right on the corner."

"Okay," Wilson said. "After my time, I guess. But there was a lot of exposed brick all through those buildings. They're old cotton warehouses, you know."

"So you wouldn't remember if there was a wall in there, separating the back from the front?" Wyatt asked.

"No." Wilson shook his head slowly. "They were all under one kind of construction or another. He was gonna put a restaurant in one of them, I think."

"There was a witness that said he saw Crawford and two other men in front of his oyster business the night he went missing," Maggie said. "Fitch. He said they seemed to be arguing. We haven't been able to locate Fitch."

"Rollie Fitch," Wilson said. "Died of cancer...oh, back in the early eighties."

"So much for that," Wyatt said. "We're wondering about this thing with Boudreaux."

"Which one?"

"Bennett."

"Which thing?"

"The alibi. Apparently, he got into a problem with Crawford at Papa Joe's that night."

"Yeah. I don't remember what it was about, though. Just words; it didn't get physical."

"But after Fitch came forward, you went to talk to Boudreaux?"

"Sure," Wilson said. He seemed a bit more wary, a bit less warm than he had when they'd walked in.

"We see in the case file that you did, and that Boudreaux supposedly had an alibi for the time Fitch thought he saw Crawford and the other guys," Wyatt said. "But there's no statement."

"Sure there is. Check the file again."

"We did," Maggie said.

Wyatt coughed into his hand. "We'll look around. Maybe it was mis-filed. What was his alibi?"

Wilson looked over at Maggie, then back to Wyatt. "I'm sorry. I honestly can't remember."

Wyatt nodded at his feet for a few seconds before looking back up at Wilson. "No offense, but there's a faint taste of crap to that."

The man stared back at Wyatt. "No offense, but I don't care what it tastes like. That was almost forty years ago."

There was an uncomfortable silence for a moment. Finally Maggie spoke up. "Did you know Bennett Boudreaux at all?"

"Not much. He'd been to town a few times, but he didn't live there then."

"What about after he moved to town? You know him much then?" Wyatt asked.

"Everybody did." Wilson seemed to put some effort into sounding less defensive or hostile. "But not back then."

"What was he like back then?" Maggie asked, and then wondered why she'd asked it.

Wilson looked at her for a moment. "About what he's like now."

"He was only twenty-two then."

The man shrugged. "He didn't have the money, the connections, the rep back then, but people were leery of him."

"Why's that?" Wyatt asked him.

"He just had that way about him. The old man was a loudmouth and a hothead, always getting into fights and so on. Bennett Boudreaux was quiet, but you knew he meant business."

"But you don't remember what his alibi was," Maggie said.

Wilson rubbed at his jaw and sighed. "Look. I'm too old and jaded for BS. One law enforcement officer to another, don't waste your time on Boudreaux. I didn't like the man, then or later. I know a lot of things he *has* done, none of which he ever got indicted for, but he didn't have anything to do with this thing."

Wyatt and Maggie looked at each other, then Wyatt sighed at Wilson. "But you won't tell us where he said he was at the time."

"And you can subpoena me if you ever come up with some wild evidence against Boudreaux, but I'll probably just forget again." He looked at his watch. "If he was a viable suspect, I'd tell you. Holden Crawford was a decent guy."

Wyatt stood, and Maggie reluctantly followed suit. "What about Mrs. Crawford?" she asked. "What was she like?"

"Beth Crawford. I haven't thought about her in years," he smiled. "Franklin County's very own Farrah Fawcett-Majors."

For some reason, that made Maggie sad. It also made her want to go back to the nursing home for a second look, because the description didn't jibe with her memory.

"Does she know yet?" Wilson asked.

"We just left her," Wyatt said. "She's in an assisted living facility now."

"You don't say. That's a shame. She was always busy, always running. He was more laid back."

"Still is," Wyatt said as he headed for the door.

⚓ ⚓ ⚓

"That really rusts my bucket," Wyatt said. "Let's all be really open about the fact that we're not gonna tell any truth here today."

Maggie pulled onto Hwy 98, then looked over at Wyatt. "You think he was taking money?"

"How the hell would I know. Let's go ask Boudreaux."

"Now?"

"Yeah, now."

Maggie chewed the edge of her lip. "Why don't you let me go?"

"No."

"I think he'll speak more freely with just me."

"I don't doubt that," Wyatt said. He took a drink of his Dew. "Nonetheless, we'll go together."

That Wyatt might not trust her to be forthcoming was actually pretty well justified. It bothered her anyway. It also bothered her that she preferred to talk to Boudreaux alone. She stared out the road for a moment.

"Say it," Wyatt said.

Maggie looked back at Wyatt. "Say what?"

"Whatever you're trying not to say."

She shrugged. "You've got every right to insist."

"So I did."

"It still bugs me."

Wyatt fiddled with the air conditioning vent for a minute before he replied. "Let's get some perspective. I'm not only your boss—the sheriff, no less—I'm also your best friend. Of course I'm going to get in between you and your pet serial killer—"

"There's nothing serial about his killings—"

"Excuse me. His run of the mill killings. In any event, the man has killed two people in the last few months, on *your* behalf I will add."

"Alessi was choking me to death!"

"And all Sport Wilmette did was stand by while Gregory Boudreaux absconded with your honor."

Wyatt stopped as he saw the look on her face. "I didn't mean that as flippantly as I said it." She nodded. "All I'm saying is that he was already a known criminal, and now we know him to be somebody who has taken enough of an interest in you to kill people."

"It's not that kind of interest."

"I didn't qualify it."

"You didn't have to. I'm telling you, he doesn't have the hots for me or whatever incorrect way you've put it before."

"He has something."

"It's platonic."

"It's weird! That's all. He's a crook and a killer. You're a cop. That makes it weirdness."

"You didn't seem especially eager to press charges against him for Alessi."

"Oh, I agreed with the sentiment, if not the method or the extreme. He cut his throat from one side to the other, Maggie."

"I know that. The freaking body washed right past me."

"Did you ever ask him how he killed Sport? I mean, before he chopped him up and threw him into the Gulf?"

"He never straight up said he did it. It was a hypothetical conversation."

"My ass."

"I never asked."

"Well, I will go with you to speak with Boudreaux, and I'll be there to make sure we don't forget to ask any important questions, okay?" Wyatt picked up a French fry.

"Fine," she said, sounding like it wasn't.

"Okee-doke," Wyatt said back, sounding like he didn't care.

CHAPTER
EIGHT

oudreaux's seafood business, Sea-Fair, was located on Water Street, right on Scipio Creek, which opened into Apalachicola Bay. Maggie's tires crunched through the oyster shell parking lot, and she parked the Jeep near the front door.

As she and Wyatt climbed out of the car, a moist breeze from the water brushed past them. Maggie looked up at the sky. There was just enough low-hanging gray to let her know they'd get their customary 3:15 shower. When she breathed in, she tasted a hint of wet metal.

They were greeted by Boudreaux's slightly-mousy blond receptionist, who seemed reluctant to call Boudreaux, but did so anyway. When she hung up, she let them know that Boudreaux was in the fish processing room and that she'd take them back. Maggie advised her back that she knew where it was and they'd find their own way. The receptionist was displeased, in an inconsequential sort of way.

Maggie and Wyatt made their way through several hallways, finally coming to the metal door where Boudreaux's crew dressed and packed grouper, snapper, and other high-demand fish for the restaurant and supermarket trade.

Wyatt knocked on the door, and it was opened a moment later by Boudreaux himself.

He was dressed in his usual manner; casual but expensively. Light-colored trousers and a blue chambray shirt hung perfectly on his still-trim frame, and his boat shoes were practical, but cost more than all of Maggie's shoes combined. As always, his thick, sandy brown hair was impeccable. He didn't look all that surprised to see them.

"Hello, Sheriff Hamilton," he said smoothly.

"Good afternoon, Mr. Boudreaux," Wyatt said politely.

Boudreaux's eyes rested a moment longer on Maggie, and he nodded at her. "Maggie."

"Mr. Boudreaux."

He opened the door wider, and stepped back to let them in.

The room was busy, noisy with the sounds of at least a dozen white-clad people dressing and butchering fish at two rows of stainless steel tables.

"I'm just packing up some fish heads to take home," Boudreaux said, indicating they should follow him.

He stopped at the nearest table, where several fish heads waited in a clear plastic bag. There were quite a few more in a bucket next to the table, and he reached down and took out two. They were redfish.

"If I don't bring some home for soup stock, Miss Evangeline starts slinging voodoo at me," he said.

"Does it work?" Wyatt asked.

"Well, I'm bringing home the fish, so I'd say it does, wouldn't you?" He smiled politely at Wyatt as he dropped the fish heads into a bag, then glanced over at Maggie. "Would you like to take some home, Maggie?"

"No, thank you," Maggie answered. "I've got plenty."

Boudreaux began twisting the bag shut. "How can I help the two of you?" he asked.

"We'd like to ask you a few questions about the building you used to own on Commerce Street."

"The florist," Boudreaux said as he made a knot in the bag.

"That and some other things. Maybe more privately?" Wyatt asked.

Boudreaux reached up to grab the nozzle of a heavy, industrial hose that hung from the ceiling. He rinsed his hands and the bag before turning back to them. The water coursed down a nearby drain in the tile floor. The same tile floor that Wyatt hadn't been permitted to tear up.

"Let's talk in my office," Boudreaux said, and led the way back to the door.

They followed him out, then down the hallway. "I assume this is about the body that was found," he said as they walked. The hall was narrow and Wyatt was abreast of Boudreaux, towering over him by almost a foot. Maggie walked behind, not towering at all.

"Why do you assume that?" Wyatt asked.

"Because that's what's going on this week. And because I used to own the building."

Boudreaux opened a door and stepped aside to let them in. Maggie had never been in Boudreaux's private office, and she was surprised that it was as impressive as it was. He tended toward understatement, but the rich mahogany furnishings and local artwork were meant to convey the money and power that he usually pretended to overlook.

Maggie and Wyatt sat down in a pair of burgundy leather armchairs as Boudreaux put the bag of fish heads into a built-in mini-fridge and then sat down behind his desk. He leaned back in the leather desk chair that looked more comfortable than Maggie's bed, and waited for one of them to speak.

"The body that was found in the flower shop last night was Holden Crawford's," Wyatt said.

"I see."

"Did you know him?"

"Of course I did," Boudreaux said calmly. "I assume you read the file." He glanced over at Maggie, and she could practically feel those blue eyes checking her bone density.

"What was the issue between you and Crawford?" she asked him.

She watched one finger scratch gently at his left eyebrow, something he did when he was choosing his words, which he always did carefully.

"In general, the issues were between him and my father," he said. "They were competitors. Between the two of them, they bought and sold ninety percent of the oysters that came out of the bay."

"What did that have to do with you?" Maggie asked.

"Not much," he answered. "But I had just graduated from Tulane, a Masters in finance. I'd started taking over the running of my father's shrimping operation back home, so I was a little more involved in his business here as well."

"Did you have dealings with Crawford?" Wyatt asked.

"Not really. But I was something of a go-between for the two of them, a role I found less than satisfying."

Maggie cleared her throat before speaking. "What happened at Papa Joc's that night? The night he disappeared?"

Boudreaux sighed softly and leaned forward onto his desk. "He was drunk. Or had been drinking. There was an event going on, what would probably be called a pub crawl these days. All of the raw bars and seafood restaurants were participating. I ran into him at Papa Joe's."

"Okay," Maggie said.

"He had some nasty things to say about my father, in a fairly loud voice," Boudreaux said. "I couldn't disagree with anything he said, but I took exception nonetheless."

"What kind of things?" Wyatt asked.

"That he underpaid for his oysters, which he did. That he undersold to the vendors to undercut Crawford, also true. That he was a bully and an ass, which he was."

"So where'd you go after Papa Joe's?" Wyatt asked casually.

Boudreaux regarded him for a moment. "I went home."

It wasn't the answer Maggie expected. "To your father's house?"

"Yes."

"Was your father there?" Wyatt asked.

"No, he was on a fishing trip that weekend."

"Huh," Wyatt said.

Boudreaux looked at him mildly. "That wasn't unusual."

"Well, the thing is, according to Bradford Wilson, you had an alibi for the time at which Crawford was seen arguing with another man in front of his business. Home alone isn't much, as alibis go."

"I suppose it isn't," Boudreaux agreed.

"So why would he say you had one?"

"Sheriff Wilson smoked a lot of pot," Boudreaux said, and Maggie could just see one corner of his lip twitching.

"Is that a fact?" Wyatt asked, as though Boudreaux had shared some mildly interesting fact about the mating habits of sandpipers.

Wyatt had a low BS threshold, and Maggie could see by the set of his jaw that he'd already breached it.

"Here's the thing," said Wyatt somewhat pleasantly. "At the time Crawford went missing, you were under some suspicion because of the argument you had with him at Papa's, and the fact that a man of similar stature was seen arguing or fighting with Crawford later. Your alibi, or the alibi Wilson says you had, was what knocked you out of the running."

He waited for Boudreaux to say something. Boudreaux waited as well.

"But now, there's the fact that you bought Crawford's business later on, including the building where his body was found," Wyatt continued. "That alibi would be even handier for you now. And you're telling me you don't have one."

"Nor do I need one," Boudreaux said quietly, as he folded his hands on the desk. "I didn't have anything to do with his disappearance, or his death. Yes, I bought his business and his property later on. It was beneficial to me, and to his wife. The business was falling apart."

"What did you do with the building?" Wyatt asked.

"For a while, it was just a tax write-off, which I needed by then," Boudreaux said. "Then I had new floors and windows put in and leased the spaces out."

"What went in there?"

"A hair salon," Maggie answered for Boudreaux. "I had my hair done there for prom."

"Yes," Boudreaux said. "Then it was a gift shop, but that went out of business fairly quickly. That was when I sold the building to the gentlemen who own it now."

Maggie had a brief memory of sitting underneath a hair dryer up against that brick wall. If she'd known what was encased just behind her, she'd have been more curious than anything else, even then.

"Let's revisit your alibi for a second," Wyatt said.

"I don't have one," Boudreaux said.

"I don't believe you," Wyatt said. "And that's problematic."

"I suppose it could be," Boudreaux said smoothly. He looked over at Maggie.

"Mr. Boudreaux," she said. "It concerns me that you won't tell us where you were or who you were with. Just clear it up."

"I apologize, Maggie."

"I tend to think you didn't have anything to do with this," she said.

Boudreaux held her stare for a moment before he spoke. "Why is that, Maggie?"

Maggie was trying to come up with an answer when Wyatt spoke up.

"Maggie says you wouldn't kill for money," Wyatt said. Maggie thought about shooting him.

"Is that right?" Boudreaux asked, smiling slightly at Maggie before he looked at Wyatt. "She's correct."

"So why *would* you?"

"Why would you?" Boudreaux countered. He sat back in his chair. "Buying Crawford's assets was an investment. It cost me money for quite some time before it actually made me any. To be truthful, I had no need of his business at the time, and my father was misguided in thinking that empty lot would help him. He just wanted to get what he wanted, whether it was a good business decision or not."

"But he didn't get it. You did," said Wyatt.

"Yes. My father passed away the year before Crawford was declared legally dead, and his wife was free to sell the business."

"Then you took over both businesses."

"Correct."

"Do you know of anyone else that might have wanted to kill Crawford?" Maggie asked.

"I don't really," Boudreaux answered. "He was a decent enough man, though a poor businessman."

"How's that?" Wyatt asked.

"He went into debt to buy that property downtown, then took out more loans to renovate it. Yet he held onto that empty lot on the waterfront. His wife nearly went bankrupt trying to keep his business afloat after he disappeared."

"But you don't know of anyone else he might have had trouble with?" Maggie asked.

"No."

"Neither do we," Wyatt said almost cheerfully.

Maggie shifted in her seat, drawing Boudreaux's attention from Wyatt to her. "Do you know which company it was that was doing the remodeling for Crawford?"

"No, I'm sorry. I don't," Boudreaux answered. "By the time I moved here in '83, they'd already done whatever they'd been doing."

"What was in there when you bought it?"

"It was being used to store antiques. Mrs. Crawford had a shop next door," Boudreaux said. "I bought this desk from her."

Maggie nodded and looked over at Wyatt, who was frowning in the general direction of Boudreaux's desk.

"So, if you bought Crawford's business, what happened to it?" Wyatt asked. "There's nothing there."

"Precisely," Boudreaux answered. "The point of buying it was so that it wouldn't exist. I do still have some of his boats and equipment. I sold that building to a developer a long time ago. They never did anything with it. I believe they've since sold it to someone else who isn't doing anything with it." He glanced at his watch and stood. "I'm sorry, but I need to get home," he said. "I'm expected at a city council dinner."

Maggie and Wyatt both stood up as well. Maggie saw the corners of Wyatt's mouth turn down. She knew it irked him that Boudreaux and his wife both sat on the city council, despite everyone knowing that he was shady. He was also good friends with half a dozen senators and congressmen. This had bugged Maggie, too, at one time. It bugged her less now, and she felt a twinge of regret for that.

"I notice your wife still hasn't come back from Louisiana," Wyatt said. Boudreaux's wife had left town just after the funeral of Boudreaux's stepson. Patrick Boudreaux had been a State's Attorney for Franklin County. He'd also been a cokehead and a criminal, who had had Maggie's ex-husband killed. Maggie had shot him dead after he'd also tried to kill Wyatt. Boudreaux hadn't seemed to hold it against her.

"No," Boudreaux said as he walked around his desk. "I'm not sure she will."

"You didn't do her in, did you?" Wyatt asked, as he took Boudreaux's proffered hand.

"No need," Boudreaux answered as he gripped Wyatt's hand then let it go.

He turned to Maggie and she held out her hand. "If you have any other questions, Maggie, I'm always available."

His grip was firm, but gentle, and Maggie felt the old oystering callouses on his palm.

"Thank you, Mr. Boudreaux," she said.

He held her hand, and her gaze, for just a moment. Those eyes. They never failed to fascinate her. "It was good to see you, Maggie."

He let go of her hand, and Maggie caught Wyatt's look of disdain as Boudreaux walked to the door and opened it for them. Maggie went through first and waited in the hall as Wyatt took his time. He stopped and turned in the doorway.

"I call bull-crap on pretty much everything that's been said here today," Wyatt said.

"That's certainly your prerogative, Sheriff," Boudreaux answered. "Ironically though, my reputation as the town villain was founded on something I *didn't* do."

He shut the door behind Wyatt, and Wyatt looked over at Maggie. "You're more polite to him than you are to me," he said.

"You don't like it when I'm polite to you," she said.

"That's because with me you don't mean it."

They were silent for a moment as they walked. Maggie could feel the irritation coming off of Wyatt.

"What's wrong?" she asked.

"You guys have conversations when you're not saying anything," Wyatt said.

"I don't know about that," Maggie said, though she wasn't sure she was telling the truth.

"Maybe you'd have to see it from my chair," Wyatt said.

NINE

Maggie and Wyatt were silent most of the way across the causeway to Eastpoint, where the Sheriff's Office was located. They then went to their separate offices to file their reports on the interviews they'd conducted that day.

At five o'clock, Maggie hitched her purse onto her shoulder and walked to Wyatt's office. The door was open, and she walked over to his desk, where he sat pecking at his computer.

"Hey," he said, without looking up.

"I'm done for the day," she said. "I sent you my report on Mrs. Crawford and Bradford Wilson."

He looked up at her. "I'm almost done with Boudreaux. I left out the creepy parts."

"It's not creepy," she said.

Wyatt sighed at her.

"Ok, it's a little creepy," she said.

"Go shut the door," Wyatt told her.

Maggie walked over and closed the door quietly, and walked back to the desk. Wyatt took off his cap and ran a hand through his hair before putting it back on.

"One of your most attractive qualities is your loyalty," Wyatt said. "He kept Alessi from killing you, and maybe killing the kids. I get that."

"Okay."

"But you're a cop. He's a crook. A dangerous crook. We know that," Wyatt said. "You know that."

"He's not dangerous to me," Maggie said quietly.

"And that's the bad part," Wyatt said.

They looked at each other for a moment. Maggie wasn't sure what to say. Wyatt was both right and wrong.

"Maggie. He's killed two men that we know of for sure. One of them watched you get raped. The other one was trying to kill you. This guy, he has some kind of thing for you. Whether or not you acknowledge it exists, it does."

"It's not what you think it is."

"I don't know what it is," Wyatt said. "The nature of it is really beside the point. What concerns me is that it's there. And whether you want to admit it or not, you like the guy."

Maggie started to protest, but she and Wyatt were better than that. "It's not a romantic thing, Wyatt."

"I know that much," he said. "We wouldn't be having this conversation if it was."

He got up and walked around the desk, then leaned back against it, his impossibly long legs stretched out in front of him.

"I'm your boss. The Sheriff," he said. "More importantly, I'm your best friend and…whatever else I am."

"Important," Maggie said.

He looked her in the eye, and there was concern and warmth and something else in his expression that brought a heat to her chest.

"No woman needs a guy like Boudreaux looking out for her, and no cop needs to feel any kind of loyalty to a guy like Boudreaux, either."

"It doesn't make him immune," she said.

"I know that. I think. All the same, it's not a good thing, Maggie. You need to step back."

"Are you taking me off the case?" she asked.

"No. I'm saying you need to regain your perspective. Personally and professionally."

"I know," Maggie said. "I'm working on it. But I don't think he killed Crawford."

"Why not? Personal feelings aside, why not?"

Maggie stared out the window for a moment, trying to nail it down herself. Finally she looked back at Wyatt.

"No need," she said, echoing Boudreaux's own words.

⚓ ⚓ ⚓

Maggie's parents lived in a modest frame house right on the bay, just outside Apalach on Hwy 98. Maggie drove down the long gravel driveway and parked in front.

Her parents had bought the house back in the early eighties, and turned a ramshackle cottage into the safe, warm home in which she'd grown up. It had been just the three of them, except for a short time after her mother's father, the former policeman, had passed away. Her grandmother had come to live with them for a few years until she, too, had passed.

The front door opened as Maggie headed for the house, and Gray Redmond stepped out onto the porch.

"Hey there, Sunshine," he said, smiling.

"Hey, Daddy."

Maggie loved her mother fiercely, but she adored her father. She'd always been a Daddy's girl. She'd gone with him out onto the oyster beds from the age of four or five, and they'd spent thousands of hours playing Scrabble, building furniture in the garage, and fishing off the dock in the back yard. Even now, if Maggie needed to talk, she needed to talk to Daddy.

Gray waited on the top step, then gave Maggie a hug. He had finally regained most of his weight after a year-long recovery from lung surgery, but he would always be a lanky man. He was six feet tall and barely more than one hundred and sixty pounds, but he'd worked the oyster beds since he was a teen, and he had the strength to show for it.

He stepped back to look at Maggie, his graying, sandy-colored hair falling over his brow. "How's my girl?"

"Good, Daddy. Did you and Kyle have fun?"

"Yeah, we've almost got that little boat ship-shape," her father answered. He and Kyle were restoring Gray's father's old oyster skiff. It had been sitting in Maggie's yard, behind the house her grandfather had built, for most of her life. Now it was going to belong to her son.

"Good," Maggie said. "It's pretty much the only thing he's talked about lately."

"Men have an innate need to build things," Gray said. "Or to un-build them."

Gray opened the door for Maggie, then followed her to the kitchen at the back of the house. Kyle was sitting at the pine table her father had built, eating a slice of cheese.

"Hey, Mom," he said when Maggie walked in.

"Hey, buddy," Maggie said. "Good day?"

"Sure." Kyle had become increasingly monosyllabic the last few months, and it bothered Maggie. She missed the enthusiasm and effusiveness of the little boy he'd been before his father had died.

"Hi, sweetie," Maggie's mother was standing at the stove, stirring a pot of soup.

"Hey, Mom," Maggie said.

Sky was the image of her mother, and Maggie was the image of hers. At fifty-eight, Georgia Redmond still had the kind of beauty that didn't require makeup, and her figure was as trim as it had been when she was Homecoming Queen. Maggie hoped that she would age half as well.

"You want to stay for dinner?" her mother asked. "I made Fisherman's Stew."

"It smells great, but I was thinking about taking Kyle for a quick ride in the runabout." She looked at her son. "Does that sound alright?"

Kyle gave a slight shrug. "Yeah, sure."

"I can pack some up for you to take home. There's plenty," Georgia said.

"Sure, that would be nice," Maggie replied. "I didn't thaw anything before I left for work."

"We read about that body that was found over at the florist," Gray said as he walked to the kitchen sink.

"That's just macabre," Georgia said, a little breathlessly. "You know, those buildings used to be part of the Underground Railroad."

"Really?" Maggie asked.

Gray started washing his hands at the sink, and spoke over his shoulder. "They have a real history from Prohibition, too."

"Do you think it was some poor slave, or a gangster?" Georgia asked.

"No, this body's not quite that historical," Maggie said. "It's Holden Crawford."

Georgia's face lost all of its excitement. She stared back at Maggie blankly. "Holden Crawford," she repeated.

"Yes." Maggie looked from her mother to her father's back. His hand washing had slowed somewhat. "Did you guys know him?"

"Sure," her father said quietly. "Somewhat."

"I'd almost forgotten all about that," Georgia said. "Are you sure it's him?"

"Yes. Larry matched his dental records."

Gray shut off the water and took a dishtowel from the hook by the sink, turned around and started drying his hands. "That's a shame," he said to the towel. "Do you know what happened to him?"

"Not yet," Maggie answered. "But he was seen arguing with some other men, or one other man, the night he went missing. Some blood was found in front of his place."

"I remember," Gray said.

Maggie glanced over at her mother, who was watching her husband, the wooden spoon she was holding dripping into the pot. Maggie looked back over at her father, who was focused on folding the dish towel.

"Did you know him, Daddy?" Maggie asked again, quietly.

Gray folded the towel again, then hung it back on the hook, where it immediately unfolded, before he looked at Maggie. "Sure. I sold him oysters when I was first starting out."

"I always kind of hoped he'd just taken off for some reason," Georgia said.

"Did you know him much, Mom?"

"Not really." Georgia laid the spoon down on a white ceramic spoon rest. "I knew Mrs. Crawford better. She was my cheerleading coach in high school."

"I didn't know that," Maggie said. "What was she like?"

"She was nice. A slave driver to us girls. You know, in a good way." Georgia wiped at a few drops of stew on the counter. "She insisted we work hard, get it right. She always wanted us to win." Georgia smiled, just a little, and shrugged. "But she was always bringing us cupcakes or making us hair bows for competitions and things. I think she probably thought of us like her daughters. They didn't have any children."

Maggie nodded and looked over at her father. He was leaning back against the counter, staring at the floor.

Gray Redmond was entirely self-educated, and he'd educated himself well. If someone mentioned a classic book, he'd not only read it, but probably owned a copy. But he was by choice a simple man.

He liked the jeans he'd broken in decades ago, worn to a flannel-like softness. He liked the music of a hand plane on old wood. He liked his Scrabble and his coffee and the stillness of the oyster beds at sunrise. Maggie's work, and the secrets of her past, had brought a darkness and a noise to Gray's life, especially in recent months, which he would have avoided if he'd had a choice.

He looked up at Maggie now. "Have you talked with his wife?"

"Yes. She knows," Maggie said.

"She's still living?" Georgia asked.

"Yes, she's in an assisted living place over in Port St. Joe," Maggie answered. "She has Alzheimer's or dementia."

"Oh. I didn't know that." Georgia looked at her husband, who nodded. "That's too bad."

Maggie looked at her father, too, and couldn't help feeling that he seemed distracted or uncomfortable. "Did you know that, Daddy?"

He looked at her. "I think I'd heard that, yes."

Maggie stared at her father a moment. "You okay, Daddy?"

He stared back at her. "Sure. It's just disturbing. I haven't thought about Crawford in years." He frowned at Maggie for a moment. "That was a long time ago. I expect you have your work cut out."

Maggie nodded. There was no real way to answer without mentioning Boudreaux, and Boudreaux was something of a sore topic between Maggie and her parents. They understandably disapproved of her talking to him much. Her mother just worried it would tarnish her reputation and possibly lead her astray somehow. Her father, on the other hand, knew that Boudreaux had killed Sport Wilmette over Maggie's rape, a rape her father had known nothing about until the past summer. He had graver concerns than did his wife.

"At the time, Bennett Boudreaux was questioned about Crawford's disappearance," she said.

Her father nodded. "I remember," he said to the floor.

Maggie caught some movement from her mother out of the corner of her eye. Her Mom had started ladling some soup into a plastic container.

"Goodness," Georgia said without turning around. "All this stuff from the past."

Maggie did the mental math and shook her head. "It's hard to imagine you being Sky's age," she said. "And I can't imagine Sky getting married."

"Well," Gray said quietly, "fortunately Sky doesn't have any reason to hurry."

Maggie knew her parents had gotten married a little ahead of schedule because she was on the way. They would have anyway, and had been madly in love ever since. Even so, the scheduling wasn't something Kyle was privy to, so she was glad when he interrupted.

"Can we go, Mom?"

Maggie looked over at him. "Yeah, sure." She wondered if the talk of bodies was bugging him. A few months ago, he would have asked questions about how the body had looked and smelled.

"Let me just pack up this stew," Georgia said, sounding a little relieved at the change in direction.

"Are we taking Dad's boat?" Kyle asked.

"Yeah," Maggie answered. "Is that cool?"

"Yeah."

Maggie looked at her father. "Thanks for letting Kyle hang out."

Gray smiled at her. "Best company I know, since you had the audacity to grow up."

Georgia walked over and held the soup out to Maggie. "Here you go, sweetie."

"Thanks, Mom," Maggie said. The container was warm in her hand, and her mouth watered just a little.

"How's Wyatt doing?" Gray asked.

"He's doing okay," Maggie answered. "We're working together on this Crawford thing." She couldn't help shrugging just a bit. "He's not crazy about me having to deal with Boudreaux much."

"Yes, well," Gray said to the floor. "We're not too wild about it, either, Sunshine."

Maggie and Kyle hugged her parents goodbye and headed out of the kitchen. On her way out, Maggie glanced over her shoulder. Her parents were staring at each other, and Maggie could only describe the look between them as a worried one.

She sighed as she followed her son to the front door. Boudreaux was an issue in every one of her relationships.

CHAPTER

TEN

When Maggie's ex-husband David had been killed in July, he'd left behind very little other than the people who had loved him.

There was the small insurance policy that had been divided between the kids' college funds, an old Toyota pickup that Sky now drove, and the little runabout that would one day belong to Kyle.

Maggie opened the throttle up a bit as Scipio Creek opened onto the bay, and steered the boat toward St. George Island, just a few miles off the mainland. Kyle sat on one of the cooler boxes behind her, and Maggie's heart clenched a little as she looked over her shoulder at him.

His black hair whipped in the wind, and his profile, as he stared out at their wake, made Maggie feel like she'd accidentally stepped into a time machine. Kyle was eleven, the same age she and David had been when they'd first met. They'd become best friends fast, been inseparable all through junior high and high school, and gotten married as soon as Maggie graduated college.

The oil spill had decimated the local shrimp population for a time, and David had lost his boat and his business. A year later, he'd started drinking, and running pot for a cousin of his. Maggie had divorced the best friend she'd ever had.

Thankfully, they'd repaired their friendship over the years, and he had been a wonderful father in many ways. Maggie still missed him so much sometimes that she stopped breathing. She wasn't sure she'd ever been in love with him, but she'd loved him deeply, and his absence was felt daily. She knew the kids were dealing with that vacancy, too.

They passed St. George and continued out for a few miles, until they got to a spot Maggie knew very well. It was the place that David had always called his "golden hole," the place he'd insisted he hauled the best loads. It was also the spot where they had spread his ashes.

She cut the engine and released the sea anchor. The relative silence was jarring, after the wind and the growling of the outboard. Maggie planted her feet as the little boat steadied itself, then walked back toward Kyle and sat down.

They sat without speaking for a few minutes, the silence broken only by the gentle slap of the waves against the boat and the cry of an occasional gull. By the time Kyle spoke, their wake had played itself out.

"Why'd we come here?" Kyle asked, mild curiosity in his voice.

Maggie shrugged, even though he was looking out at the water. "I come out here sometimes, when I miss your Dad. I talk to him."

"He's not here," he said matter-of-factly.

Maggie felt something punch at her chest. "I know. It just seems like the right place to do it."

Kyle nodded, but didn't answer. She waited for him to speak again, then decided conversation was up to her.

"I know you miss your Dad."

"Yeah."

"We all do."

Kyle nodded, and they sat for a moment. Maggie had always found it so easy to talk to Kyle, much easier than talking to Sky, just as it had always been so easy to talk to David. But some things just didn't get said with ease.

"Ever since I was your age," Maggie said finally, "whenever I needed some advice, or just some peace, I would go out on the oyster beds with your Granddad."

"I know."

"If you ever want to come out here, I'll bring you."

Kyle waited a moment before answering. "Okay."

Sky was Maggie's firstborn, and the older she got, the more she became Maggie's friend. But Kyle was the love of Maggie's life. He was gentle and kind, goofy and wise. He opened doors for women and the elderly, and brought Maggie flowers from the woods.

Now and again, he would still slow dance with her in the kitchen when a good song came on the radio. Maggie felt his hurt, always, and her instinct was always rescue.

"I'm sorry he's not here anymore. To be with," she said quietly.

Kyle looked at her finally, tried to smile. "Me, too."

They sat in silence again for a few moments, then Kyle spoke up.

"Hanging out with Wyatt helps sometimes," he said, twisting at a blue braided bracelet.

"Yeah?"

"Yeah. I mean, it's not like you just met him. I've known him my whole life. He's a good guy."

"Yeah."

Kyle swallowed, then looked over at her. "Dad liked him, too."

"I know," she said, and something like guilt swirled through her stomach.

"He said you guys would probably end up getting married," Kyle said matter-of-factly.

It took Maggie a few seconds to answer. "Well. I mean, we're...we haven't even thought about stuff like that," she said. "We're barely dating."

Kyle nodded, looked back out at the water. "Well, you guys should probably step it up a little. Life is short."

Maggie wasn't sure how to respond to that, she was so taken aback. But then Kyle looked at her and gave her another small smile, and she thanked God for his existence. She smiled back at him.

"Our jobs, Kyle. You know."

"Yeah, I know. But still. You're not doing anything wrong."

"Well, it's complicated, you know?"

"Mom, *every*thing is complicated."

Maggie smiled out at the water. "That is a fact, little man."

Then they sat for some time, not speaking anymore, both of them lost in their own thoughts, and their own conversations with a man who had left them before anyone was ready.

⚓ ⚓ ⚓

Maggie knew she had seen the name of the construction company that had done Crawford's renovations, and she was rifling through the case file the next morning when she was interrupted by the bleating of her cell phone. She looked at it and saw it was Larry Davenport.

"Hey, Larry," she answered.

"Good morning, Maggie," he answered in his gravelly, constantly distracted way. "I have some news of import to share."

"What's that?"

"I believe we can establish cause of death for Mr. Crawford. Would you like to hear it over the phone or are you going to drop by here to see for yourself, as you generally insist on doing?"

"I'll come in," she said.

"I imagined you would," he said. "Perhaps you'd be kind enough to stop and get me an Earl Grey."

"I can do that," Maggie answered. "Non-fat milk and one honey?"

"Alas," was his answer.

Maggie hung up the phone and flipped through a few more pages until she found the one she'd been looking for. Back in 1977, a deputy had noted that the building on Commerce Street had been checked for signs of Crawford, with an escort from Bayside Contracting to make sure no one got conked by a falling beam.

She swung around to her computer and did a search, but found nothing on Bayside Contracting. She picked up her phone and called a friend at the building department. Three phone calls later, she knew that the company had closed in the nineties, but she had the phone number of the owner's widow, who lived on the west side of town.

She hung up and grabbed her things, walked down to Wyatt's office. He was standing behind his desk, draining the last of his café con leche. It would probably be replaced momentarily by a bottle of Mountain Dew.

"Hey," Maggie said as she walked in.

"Hey," he said back.

"Larry has some news on cause of death," she said. "You want to go over there with me?

"I can't. I have court," Wyatt answered, tossing the cup in the trash. "Besides, you know I get traumatized when Larry starts prodding and fondling the dead people."

Maggie smiled. "It's fascinating."

"*Nova* is fascinating. Autopsies are scary."

"How did you get into this line of work again?"

"By being a really clumsy running back," Wyatt answered as he walked around his desk. "I'll walk out with you."

The heartless morning sunshine blasted them in the eyes as they walked outside, and they both pulled out their sunglasses. There was a strong breeze, but it was warm even for October, even in the Panhandle, and there wasn't a cloud in the sky.

Wyatt was parked next to Maggie, and they both opened their doors and waited for their interiors to cool off a minute before getting in. Wyatt leaned on the roof of his cruiser.

"Tell Larry I'm sorry I missed it," he said.

"I'll do that," she said. "I have to stop at Delores's and get him some Earl Grey tea."

"I hope he's not using it as some kind of anti-aging thing," Wyatt said. "He's pushing eighty and looks closer to a hundred."

"You're such a jerk," Maggie said.

Wyatt waggled his eyebrows at her. "You want to kiss me anyway," he said.

Maggie felt her face heat up, and she looked away and smiled. "I do."

Wyatt grinned. "It's so adorable the way you turn red like that."

He started to get into his car. "Hey," Maggie said. He straightened back up. "Do you want to come over for dinner tonight?"

"I don't know. What are you making?"

"Garlic chicken."

"What time?"

"Whenever you want to come over. Dinner'll be ready around six."

"The kids gonna be there?"

"Yeah."

"Will there be furtive kissing? 'Cause I like it when it's furtive."

"You're twelve," she said, and climbed into her car.

L arry's office and the morgue were located in a warren in the back of the first floor of Weems Memorial Hospital, not far from downtown. Maggie took Larry's tea and her fresh *café con leche* with her, and found Larry hunched over his desk, making handwritten notes to a file. He looked up as she entered.

"Ah, good morning, Maggie," he said.

"Hi, Larry." She set the paper cup of tea on his desk.

"Thank you, my dear," he said. He lifted the lid and breathed in the aroma of the tea before putting the lid back on and taking a sip. "I miss my coffee most profoundly," he said, eyeing her cup.

"Is that the Crawford file?" she asked, gesturing at the papers in front of him.

"Sadly, no. This is a heart attack. Thirty-nine years old," he said, rising from his chair. "Terrible shame. Shall we take a peek at Mr. Crawford?"

Maggie followed Larry down a short hallway to the lab. There were four covered bodies on stainless steel tables, and Larry led Maggie to the closest one. When he folded the sheet down to the hips, Maggie saw that the chest cavity had been opened, as well as a large incision in the lower abdomen.

The body of Holden Crawford was quite different from other bodies Maggie had seen in this place. There were no fluids, and the organs were desiccated and hard, nearly unrecognizable to Maggie's only moderately trained eye.

"Let us get right to that which is relevant to you this morning," Larry said. He set his tea down on a nearby cart, then bent over the body with a long stainless steel pick.

"I've left the organs *in situ* for the moment, so you can see what I've found thus far." He poked at the opening he'd made in the parchment-like abdomen. "If you look here, you'll see that there are several cuts to the flesh of the abdomen. They're not as easy to see with the naked eye as they would be on a fresh cadaver, but they're there."

Maggie bent close to the abdomen until she could see one of the cuts he was indicating. "How many are there?"

"I've found four," Larry answered. He lifted a large flap of the abdominal skin and used the pick to gently tap at the shriveled liver. "Two of them correspond to wounds to the liver, here and here. This wound here also corresponds to a mark on the lower side of one of the ribs. You can just see it here."

He pointed with the pick, and Maggie bent lower and squinted at the underside of the rib.

"It's not particularly clear at the moment," Larry said. "The bones will need to be cleaned to get a good look at the marks and take measurements, but I believe I'll find more of them. It's quite difficult to puncture the liver without nicking a rib."

Maggie straightened up and took a sip of her coffee. "So you think he was stabbed?"

"Thoroughly. As I said, I've found four wounds thus far, but I expect that I might find more."

Maggie looked at the body for a moment. "They're fairly close together."

"Yes."

"If he had fallen or even bent very much, they'd be more spaced out." Maggie said. "So these wounds were made in quick succession, right?"

"Quite."

"Someone was either very angry, or they panicked," Maggie said, speculating aloud. "Sometimes people are so surprised that they actually stabbed someone that they do it again and again. Like they can't go back, so they want to make sure it's fatal."

Larry didn't respond, just took a sip of his tea.

"What else can you tell me so far?" Maggie asked him.

"Well, the wounds have a slightly upward trajectory, but the liver is quite high. If the assailant were roughly the same height as Mr. Crawford, I would expect the wounds to be lower in the abdomen, or at less of an angle. So I think it's safe to say the person who did this was significantly shorter than Mr. Crawford. Based on his height, I'd say somewhere between five-six and five-nine."

"Why not a taller man, thrusting fairly straight from the elbow?"

"The angle would be quite different, I think," Larry answered. "Also, the person who did this was left-handed."

Maggie tilted her head and looked at the body, thought about the second man who had been seen with Crawford that night. "It could have been a taller, right-handed man, attacking from behind, couldn't it?"

"Again, the angle. In that instance, it still would have been more severe."

Maggie nodded. "Okay."

"Mr. Crawford will be heading to Tallahassee this afternoon," Larry said. "They're much better able to examine a body of this vintage. I'll let you know what they find, but I thought this might be a helpful beginning."

"Yes," Maggie said. "It's a start."

⚓ ⚓ ⚓

The crime scene techs had given the "all clear" on the flower shop, so Maggie let William and Robert know that she was going to take one more look around and then return their place of business to them. She tended to want a last "feel" of a crime scene before it returned to being whatever it had been prior.

The day was once again unseasonably warm and, as Maggie parked in front of the shop, she hoped they would soon see what passed for autumn in the Panhandle.

A few fall tourists checking out the shop windows watched her as she yanked the crime scene tape from the door and fumbled with the lock. She was used to people rubbernecking at crime scenes, but there were still times when she felt like they were blaming her for the fact that there *was* a crime scene.

She shrugged off her innate sense of guilt and entered the shop, closing and locking the door behind her.

It was odd to be in the shop alone. She'd been a customer many times, of both the flower shop and the hair salon, but she'd never been the only person in the building. The solitude made the silence quieter, the dark corners more shadowy. It wasn't so much that there had been a body there—Maggie was used to being where bodies had been—she just didn't do alone very well, no matter where she was. A remnant of her past.

She turned on the overhead lights and walked around the cash register counter. Most of the brick wall had been removed, along with the two-by-fours that had framed Crawford in somewhat. Maggie knew they'd been stained with Crawford's bodily fluids as he'd decomposed. They'd probably remain in some evidence locker somewhere, or perhaps be donated to some place where people like her learned about two-by-fours that had been stained by decomposing bodies.

She stood in front of the hole where Crawford had been, and stared at it for a while. She could now see clear through to the room beyond the wall. She stepped inside the space, then turned around to face the main room of the flower shop, much as Crawford had. She looked up, and around her, at what remained of the wall, then turned and stepped into the room beyond it.

Apparently, the room was mainly used for storage. There were several shelving units lined with vases, shopping bags, wrapping paper and other supplies. Along one wall were two coolers filled with jars and boxes of blooms, some of them past their prime.

Maggie stepped back through the hole in the wall and dusted some mortar from her jeans. The hair dryers had stood here, back when this was a salon. Maggie thought back, tried to remember getting her hair done for prom, the only time she'd ever sat beneath one of the odd-looking machines.

She moved a few steps to the right of the hole. Here; she'd sat here, less than three feet from Crawford's corpse, wishing she could skip the baby blue satin dress, that she and David could just grab a six pack of RC and go out on Daddy's boat instead. They'd gone to the prom. Both of them had hated it.

Maggie stood behind the counter and looked toward the windows. She had no way of knowing whether there had been blinds or shades on the windows back in 1977. How much privacy had there been in this room when someone had been building—and filling—a wall?

There was a building housing several shops across the street. Directly across from the flower shop was a store that sold expensive clothing and accessories with a coastal flair. It had been there at least since she was about twenty. She couldn't remember what it had been before that.

She walked to the front of the shop, her hiking boots thumping against the beautiful new bamboo floors, and pulled the string to lift one set of blinds. The sight of William and Robert staring in at her made her lungs shrivel for just a moment. She took a deep breath and let it out slowly, then went out to the sidewalk.

"Are you done?" William asked her without preamble, smoke swirling out of his nostrils.

"Yes, I think so," she answered.

Robert heaved a sigh of relief. "Good, because we can't afford to stay closed like this."

Maggie handed him the keys to the shop.

"Sorry, guys," she said. "It's all yours."

"Is there somebody we can call, like a real *Sunshine Cleaning* company?" William asked. "Because I need Amy Adams to come deal with this."

Maggie hesitated a moment before answering, unsure if he was joking. Judging by the expectancy on his face, he was not. "There's a company in Tallahassee. I can get the name for you, if you really need me to."

"It's okay, William," Robert said. "We just go in and bleach the snot out of everything."

"It's not okay," William told him before looking at Maggie. "I am not smitten with the idea of going in there with my little Magic Eraser, scrubbing away at smears of who knows what."

"There's really nothing there," Maggie said. "The crime scene techs took anything with any evidence on it." She rethought that for a second. "There may be some stained bricks, I don't know. But honestly, you're not facing anything awful."

Robert jingled the keys in his hand like he was weighing them. "I'm going to go assess the situation," he said, heading for the door.

"I'm going to finish my cigarette," William said.

"Okay, but then let's get this over with," Robert said. He opened the door, but didn't go in. Maggie sensed he was stalling a moment. "We'll finish taking down the wall, reopen the shop, and once we've made up some of the money we've lost, we're going down south for a few days to recover."

"We're *not* going to Key West," William said firmly. Robert waved him off, then went inside and closed the door. William exhaled a plume of smoke, then looked at Maggie. "All those gays get on my final nerve."

Maggie didn't smile, but it took some effort.

"I see," she said.

TWELVE

aggie was setting the table out on the side deck when Wyatt pulled up out front. She would have known it was him by the sound of his truck, but Coco's keening and groaning as she raced around to the stairs was a dead giveaway.

Maggie walked around the corner as Coco dissolved at Wyatt's feet in the gravel driveway. Stoopid came flapping around the other corner and immediately began breakdancing his way down the stairs. He was halfway down when Wyatt and Coco were halfway up, and seemed disgusted that he had to turn around and retrace his steps.

Wyatt reached the deck and gave Coco's head one last scratch before looking at Maggie. "Hey," he said.

"Hey."

Wyatt and Maggie had been close friends, buddies really, for so long that their new relationship was still sometimes awkward. It didn't always feel natural to kiss or to hold each other until they were actually doing it. They still fumbled a bit at the moments when people who had started out as a couple would normally hug or kiss.

This was one of those moments, and when Wyatt gave her a half smile and held out an arm, Maggie felt self-conscious and clumsy until she was actually up against his chest. Then the uneasiness drifted away. It was replaced by a sense of peace, and an underlying, more subtle chaos.

Maggie lifted her face and accepted a kiss that tasted of Mountain Dew and mouthwash and sincerity, and was almost glad when she heard Sky's voice pop up from the front door.

"Put a lid on it; teenager on deck," Sky said.

Wyatt pulled away from Maggie, but left an arm wrapped around her waist.

"Hiya, Sky," he said.

"Hey, Sheriff," Sky said as she came out onto the deck. "Mom, can we have a few extra bucks to grab a burger on the way?"

"Why don't you just eat with us before you go?" Maggie asked.

"We don't have time."

"I thought you guys were hanging out with us," Wyatt said.

Sky tossed him a grin capped with slightly-rolled eyes. "Yeah, as much as we like watching you guys watching each other, we're gonna bail," she said.

"*The Martian*," Maggie told Wyatt.

"Yeah, and it's already been out for like ten minutes, and little nerd man is in there practically vibrating out of his clothes," Sky said.

"The show from the sixties?" Wyatt said.

"You need to bone up on popular culture," Sky said.

"Science geek nirvana," Maggie explained to Wyatt.

"Okeydokey," he said.

Kyle came out onto the deck, the anxiousness coming off of him in waves. "Sky, are you ready?"

"Yeah, dude, hang on," she said, then looked at Maggie.

"Go ahead," Maggie said. "My purse is on the table."

"Cool." Sky disappeared back into the house and Kyle gave Wyatt a wave.

"Hey, Wyatt," he said.

"Hey, Kyle, how's it going?"

"Okay."

Maggie pulled away from Wyatt. "I'm gonna go make sure Sky doesn't break me," she said, and maneuvered around Stoopid to get to the door. Coco was content to sit at Wyatt's feet, gazing up at him like he was the inventor of the tennis ball.

Maggie opened the screen door, and used her bare foot to gently sweep at Stoopid, who was excited about her plan to go indoors, where the refrigerator was kept.

"Not you, Stoopid," Maggie said, and slapped the door shut behind her.

Wyatt watched Stoopid walk huffily over to the wood pile and hop atop it, then he looked over at Kyle.

"So, what are you doing with yourself now that baseball season's over?"

Kyle shrugged a little. "Not much. Working on my Minecraft mods, skateboarding a little. Reading."

"Did you finish that James Lee Burke I gave you?"

"Yeah. I'm ready for the next one," Kyle said. "Robicheaux's a cool guy."

"Burke makes you feel like you're right there in Louisiana, doesn't he?"

"Yeah. I want to go to New Iberia sometime," Kyle said. "I looked at some of those places on Google Earth. It's cool 'cause they're real places."

"Your Mom loves Louisiana," Wyatt said.

"Yeah, I know. Mom and Dad got Coco there when I was little."

Coco smiled at Kyle in that way she did, and Wyatt gave her a pat.

"Maybe we could drive over there for a few days," Wyatt said. "When you're out of school."

"You and me?" Kyle asked.

"The two of us, all of us. Whichever," Wyatt said.

"That'd be pretty awesome."

Kyle looked out at the yard, his face gone a bit wistful, and Wyatt wondered if he was thinking about his father.

"You know, I was a football guy, not a baseball player like your dad," Wyatt said, "but if you want to practice, stay in shape, I know enough to throw the ball around with you."

Kyle looked back at Wyatt. It took him a moment to answer, and Wyatt thought he was going to say something about only practicing with his dad.

"I need to work on my swing," he said instead.

"I can pitch," Wyatt said.

Kyle shrugged at him a little shyly. "Okay."

"Okay," Wyatt said back.

"Dude, let's hit it," Sky said as she hurried back out the door.

"See you later, Wyatt," Kyle said as he followed Sky down the stairs.

"See you later," Wyatt said.

Sky waved over her shoulder, then Wyatt watched them climb into David's old Toyota truck and head up the driveway. He'd known Sky since she was in second grade, and it still felt weird to see her driving.

He watched them go, scratching at Coco's ear, until Maggie came back out with a platter of chicken and roasted vegetables.

"Dinner's ready, she said, and he followed her to the table.

"That smells amazing," he said.

"My grandmother's Chicken with Forty Cloves of Garlic," Maggie said as she set it on the table. "Her mother was from Normandy. Sit down."

Wyatt waited for Maggie to sit, then pulled out his chair and did the same. Coco settled democratically between them, trying to look like she wasn't hoping someone would overturn the table.

Maggie filled their plates while Wyatt poured the wine she'd opened, and they settled in to eat.

"This is freakishly good," Wyatt said after a couple of bites.

"Thank you."

"I was starving," he said.

"You've been starving for ten years," she said.

"It is pretty chronic," he agreed. He looked over at the deck railing as Stoopid flapped up to it and tapped over to peer at the table.

"Go away, Stoopid," Maggie said without enthusiasm.

Wyatt watched Stoopid warily as Stoopid watched him take another bite. "Does he know this is chicken?" Wyatt asked after he'd chewed and swallowed.

"I'm not sure he knows *he's* chicken," Maggie answered.

"This isn't one of his women, is it?"

"Are you kidding? I don't eat my chickens. I raise them for manure and eggs. And company."

Wyatt continued watching Stoopid, who was investigating Wyatt's plate in that head-tilted, one-eyed way that chickens will. Maggie plucked a piece of roasted carrot from her plate and put it on the railing, which pleased Stoopid to no end.

"You have an odd relationship with your rooster," Wyatt said.

"All of my relationships are odd," she said.

"Thank you."

Maggie ate a bite of turnip before she spoke again. "I ordered Stoopid through the mail. He was a week old when I got him. When he came, he was kind of sick, so I may have coddled him a little. He slept on my chest for the first week he was here."

Wyatt looked at her for a moment. "I can see the healing potential in that," he said, straight-faced.

"Are we already at the point in the evening where you try to irritate me?"

"It's almost effortless, really," he answered.

Maggie sighed, and they ate in silence for a moment. There was a good breeze coming off of the river, and it rustled through the live oaks and pines, danced through the Capiz shell chimes that hung outside the living room window. The air smelled of riverbed and leaves and garlic.

"Speaking of irritation," Wyatt said after a few minutes. "I did some digging around on Boudreaux today. Both Boudreauxes, actually."

Maggie paused before forking up a piece of chicken. "Yeah?"

"Yeah. Bradford Wilson seriously downplayed Bennett Boudreaux's reputation back then."

"In what way?"

"That whole 'quiet but intimidating' thing. There was more to it than that."

"Okay."

"I talked to Murphey Carmichael on the phone," Wyatt said.

Maggie knew Murph. He'd been with Apalach PD at the same time as her grandfather. Now he was in his eighties, selling pallet shelves at farmer's markets and craft shows.

"He said that Boudreaux got into a thing with some guy I don't know, earlier that summer," Wyatt said. "Over a girl. Apparently, the girl had eyes for Boudreaux and the guy didn't like it. The guy jumped Boudreaux out at the marina, and Boudreaux damn near killed him."

"Why isn't that on Boudreaux's record?"

"Because the guy was on probation and was carrying," Wyatt answered. "He never reported it, but everybody knew about it."

"Boudreaux beat up a man who was carrying a gun?"

"Apparently so."

Maggie busied herself for a moment with cutting some chicken.

"I also did some checking with Terrebonne Parish PD," Wyatt said. "Boudreaux had a juvenile record. Sealed. That wasn't in the fax they sent the Sheriff's Office in '77."

Maggie poked at her food. "You're spending a lot of time with Boudreaux," she said eventually.

"So are you," Wyatt replied.

They looked at each other for a moment, and the teasing and joking were clearly behind them.

"Not lately," Maggie said.

"Nevertheless." Wyatt had stopped eating.

"I'm worried that you're focusing too much on Boudreaux," Maggie said quietly. "That you're assuming he had something to do with Crawford because that's what you'd like to be true."

"Sure, I'd love to nail him for something from thirty-something years ago, since we haven't nailed him for anything since," Wyatt said. "But I'm focusing on Boudreaux partly because it's the most likely scenario, and partly because I'm afraid you won't. Because you *don't* want that to be true."

No, she didn't. Known killings aside, Maggie would prefer to believe that Boudreaux was innocent of this particular crime, that there were things he *hadn't* done. Things that could somehow balance the things he had, and make it more okay for her to respect and even like him. Make it alright for her to feel grateful to him, and a little obligated.

"I'm staying objective," she said. "I'm open to the possibility that he was involved, but I'm not as enthusiastic about it as you are."

"I'm sure you're not," Wyatt said. "But we're going to have to yin-yang each other on this one."

"I understand," she said. "But I feel like it's too simple, Boudreaux being the answer."

"No, simple would be if the spouse was behind it, like they usually are." Wyatt took a sip of wine. "But the case file says Mrs. Crawford was with her sick sister out off of Gibson Road. Also, no motive anyone could find. Then there was Fitch's statement."

"Even so," Maggie said. "I know you feel like I'm advocating for Boudreaux, and I know that's a problem for you personally—it is for me, too—but it doesn't seem all that likely to me."

She looked away from him, unwilling to see him looking at her like she was headed for disillusionment.

Wyatt watched her for a moment, as she stared out at the trees beyond her yard. "Try not to look so crestfallen," he said. "Boudreaux is a problem between us, but we've handled worse."

Maggie looked back at him as he leaned his elbows on the table and sighed. "Okay," she said.

"One of the benefits of being very close friends before becoming romantically involved is that we can roll with the hard stuff a little more easily," he said.

"I hope so," Maggie said, her brain snagging on the word *romantically*.

"Okay, let's forget about work for the night," he said, stabbing at a carrot. "This is why we suck at dating."

Maggie smiled, relieved to be done with the talk of Boudreaux. It made her examine herself too closely, and she'd never cared for that much.

Wyatt smiled across the table at her. "Let's enjoy our dinner and our wine, and talk about fun things," he said. "Like how bad I feel about all that sexual tension you're battling."

CHAPTER

THIRTEEN

Maggie's cell phone rang at 5:30am. She would have been more annoyed if it hadn't been preceded seven minutes earlier by the sound of Stoopid scrambling onto the window sill and coughing up a chicken lung.

She picked the phone up from the nightstand and saw it was her father.

"Hey, Daddy," she said.

"Hey, Sunshine," he said quietly. Daddy was always up by five, but Maggie's mother lazed in bed until seven. "You want to go out for a little bit?"

Maggie rubbed at her face. "Sure. I have to be in at eight."

"Then you should get a move on," he said, and hung up.

Maggie slid her legs off of the bed and headed for the bathroom.

⚓ ⚓ ⚓

Maggie and Gray said very little to each other as they stowed the lines and got underway. They spent more of their relationship in comfortable silences than they did in conversation, though when they did talk, it tended to be meaningful.

Before the sun was fully up, they reached one of Gray's favorite spots, where the bay was less than six feet deep and the gulls and the pelicans were their only company. Gray worked the tongs, his sinewy arms manipulating the long handles efficiently, without any extraneous movement, feeling the bottom for clusters of oysters, then swinging them over the side and onto the deck of the small oyster skiff.

Maggie culled the oysters, tossing out empty shells, rocks, and other debris, then chipping the oysters apart and cleaning them off. After a short time, they had a decent number, and Gray shucked the oysters while Maggie cleaned off the wooden platform and sliced a lemon.

When he had more than two dozen sweet, plump oysters on the half shell arranged on the platform, Maggie grabbed a couple of orange juices from the cooler and popped them open. Then they each chose one particularly nice-looking oyster, squeezed on some lemon, raised their shells to each other, and slurped.

Maggie closed her eyes as the brine filled her mouth first. The oysters were saltier this year. Cities upriver, particularly Atlanta, continued to pull fresh water from the Apalachicola River, throwing off the perfect balance of fresh water and salt that made Apalach oysters so special.

Maggie swallowed the water, then gently bit down on the flesh. It was sweet and tender and tasted like home.

When she opened her eyes, her father nodded at her and smiled, as he always did. They ate a few more before he spoke.

"You know, I think people undervalue the peace that comes from things that remain the same," he said.

"How do you mean?"

"People are always rushing to get the newest product, try the newest thing, move to a new house, a new country." He squeezed some lemon onto an oyster and swallowed it whole. "There's a significance to continuity that I think people overlook."

"I can see that," Maggie said.

He sat and looked at her for a moment, squinting in the brightening day. "Take you, for instance, sitting there with your oysters, just like you did when you were five and twelve and seventeen."

Maggie smiled at him as she took another sweet oyster into her mouth. He watched her eat it, his face pensive and thoughtful.

"I appreciate it, too, Daddy," she said when she'd finished. "Mornings like this grounded me. So did you."

He nodded, and looked out at the bay for a moment.

"How was your dinner with Wyatt last night?" he asked.

"Good. It was a nice night," she said.

"You need some of those," Gray said.

"Yes."

He took a drink of orange juice. "And your case?"

Maggie shrugged, scratched at the back of an oyster shell. "Wyatt and I seem to be on opposite sides of it."

"How's that?"

"He's pretty convinced that Boudreaux killed Crawford. I'm not."

Gray picked up his knife and poked at a corner of the platform with it. "I thought Boudreaux was cleared of all of this way back then, when Crawford was missing."

Maggie wasn't surprised that Gray would know that Boudreaux had been cleared. Everybody knew everything in Apalach.

"That's a bit of a snafu there," she said. "Supposedly he had an alibi, but either there's paperwork missing or the details were never in the file. There's nothing about who or what the alibi was."

Gray continued to worry the wood with the tip of his knife. "Did you ask him?"

"Yes. He says he doesn't have an alibi," she answered.

Gray squinted up at her, then used his knife to pluck an oyster from its shell and put it in his mouth.

"What do you two think about that?' he asked after he'd swallowed.

"Wyatt thinks he never had an alibi," Maggie said.

"And you?"

"I think he's lying."

"Why would he do that?" Gray asked.

Maggie tossed a shell into the water and watched it sink. "How would I know?" she asked, irritation creeping into her voice. She looked at her father. "I know you think I've gotten too close to Boudreaux, and maybe I have, but that doesn't mean I understand him."

"That's encouraging," Gray said quietly.

They sat in silence for a few moments, each inside their own heads.

"Margaret Anne, you've been raised to have sense. Just see you don't lose track of it," Gray said after a bit.

"I won't," Maggie said, though it was reassurance more than conviction.

"I sold oysters to Boudreaux for a lot of years," he said. "Not much choice, once Crawford's was closed. He was always fair; he paid well and he respects men who work the Gulf. But that doesn't mean I want him around my daughter."

"Yet you called *him* to come check on me during the hurricane," Maggie said.

"I knew he hadn't evacuated. He never has."

Maggie studied her father's face. Gray studied the water.

"Well, I'm glad you did," she said.

One moment, she'd been staring up at Alessi as he choked the life from her just inches away from her children. The next moment, Boudreaux was there, those blue eyes icy and hard as he pulled Alessi from her and out into the storm in what seemed like one motion. He'd cut Alessi's throat right there in her yard.

Maggie squeezed some lemon onto her last oyster and ate it. Then she tossed the shell over the side and sighed at her father.

"Maybe he didn't need to kill Alessi; maybe he did," she said. "But Wyatt wasn't especially anxious to charge him for it. He was defending a woman, a law enforcement officer. But he'd be pretty happy to nail him for something that happened almost forty years ago."

"Maggie, I won't pretend I'm not glad he did what he did," Gray said. "But that makes two men he killed on your account, and that's something that you should keep uppermost in your mind."

"I'll admit that Boudreaux has some pretty extreme ideas about dishonor and all that," Maggie said. "Right and wrong. But what would you have done if you'd known about Sport Wilmette?"

"I'd have killed him, most likely," Gray said. "And if Gregory Boudreaux hadn't already blown his head off, I'd have killed *him* twice." He poked the knife into the wood. It stayed there. "But I'm your dad."

"The past seems to be a theme this year, Daddy. Mine. Boudreaux's. It's a little wearying."

Gray was scooping up his empty shells from the platform. "That's the funny thing about the past, Sunshine," he said. "It's never very far behind you."

He tossed the shells overboard, and father and daughter watched them sink to the bottom, where they would soon provide a foundation for a new generation of oysters.

⚓   ⚓   ⚓

Late that afternoon, Maggie and Wyatt took separate cars to the home of Vincent Jeffries, the former best friend of the late Holden Crawford. Maggie followed Wyatt to the small home on Maple Street, and they pulled into a short drive lined with hibiscus and Florida holly.

Wyatt got out and waited for Maggie to join him, then they walked up to the door and knocked.

The man who answered was about six feet tall, but his hunching posture made him seem smaller. He wore a brown sweater against the barely perceptible autumn air, and was probably the only person in Apalach who had his heat on inside. Maggie walked in and was immediately sorry they weren't talking outside.

Everyone made their introductions, then Jeffries led them through a living room full of dark furniture, every surface of which was jammed with those collectible dolls that Maggie had never understood. Jeffries saw her eyeing them.

"My wife's," he said with a dismissive wave. "I always hated those things, but now I can't bring myself to get rid of 'em."

Jeffries took them into a kitchen at the back of the house and invited them to sit at the table. He dumped a mean-looking, fat orange cat from one of the chairs and took its place. "Hers, too," he said.

Once they were settled, he looked at Wyatt and Maggie in turn. "What can I tell y'all?"

"Well, we're trying to find out a little bit more about the night Holden Crawford went missing," Wyatt answered. "You went out with him that night?"

"Yeah, just for a little bit," Jeffries answered. "Then I came home and watched *Kojak* with Eleanor. She wasn't much for going out."

"You remember what you watched?" Maggie asked. "I wouldn't."

"Your best buddy didn't go missing that night," he said, without being rude about it. Maggie nodded.

"But you were out with Crawford when he had his run-in with Bennett Boudreaux," Wyatt said. Jeffries' statement had been in the file.

"Yeah, sure. At Papa Joe's," the old man said.

"Can you tell us more about what that was about?" Wyatt asked.

"Well, Holden and Boudreaux—Alban Boudreaux—they'd been going at it for a while. It was getting kind of heated." Jeffries took a sip from a watered down glass of tea. "Y'all want some tea?"

They both declined, and Jeffries set his glass down on the Formica table. "I'll be the first to admit that Holden was a little intoxicated that night. Not plastered, but he'd had a few. He'd seemed kind of upset the last few days or so, you know, tense, so he knocked back a few drinks that night."

"Do you know what he was upset about?" Maggie asked.

"No, he didn't want to talk about it," Jeffries said. "I knew he would eventually, so I let it go."

Maggie watched something like regret pass over the man's sun-spotted face.

"Anyway, like I said, he was a little tipsy and he'd been having a bad week, so I'll admit he kind of started what went on with him and Bennett Boudreaux."

"What happened?" Wyatt asked.

"Well, Boudreaux came in alone, ordered a bottle of beer, and Holden started in talking about Alban, you know, loud enough for Boudreaux to hear."

"What was he saying?' Maggie asked.

"Oh, that Alban was a jerk, though maybe not in such nice words," Jeffries answered. "That he was a crook. Everybody knew that already, but everybody was listening anyway."

"Then what happened?" Wyatt asked.

"Well, I had to pee, but when I came back, Boudreaux was over there with Holden, and they were having words. Boudreaux basically told him to watch his mouth and Holden was kind of itching for a fight about it, though he wasn't much of a fighting man." Jeffries stared at the water ring his glass had made on the yellow Formica, then looked back up at them. "It was the alcohol and whatever stress he was under, you know? Holden was a pretty peaceable guy."

"Gotcha," Wyatt said. "So what happened then? Somebody break it up?"

"No...no, Boudreaux warned him to be more polite or have better manners when he was talking about his family, something like that. Then he left."

"Did you and Mr. Crawford leave there together?" Maggie asked.

"No. No, I'm sorry to say I went home just a little while after that."

"Wasn't Holden drinking? You didn't give him a ride somewhere?" Wyatt asked him.

The old man seemed to get irritated pretty quickly over that. "Well, no, but he was on foot. A lot of people were," he said. "Everybody was walking up and down Water Street, all around in there. Heck, Holden just lived right over there on 4th Street. It was an easy walk. He wasn't snockered or anything."

Wyatt nodded. "Okay, so Boudreaux left and that was it?"

"Yeah, that was pretty much it. And good thing, you know, because it could have been ugly."

"How do you mean?" Maggie asked.

"Well, Boudreaux was kind of a scary guy, even back then," Jeffries said. "You guys know about what happened with that Miller kid?"

"Who?" Wyatt asked.

"I can't think of his first name," Jeffries said. "He got into a fight with Boudreaux over at Scipio Creek Marina."

"Right, right," Wyatt said. "We heard something about that. What was the deal with that?"

"Well, I wasn't there, but everybody knew about it, everybody talked about it," the old man said. "Miller was a creep, and he was a big guy, so no sympathy there for him, but people said Boudreaux was a hell of a lot scarier."

"What happened?" Maggie asked.

"I don't remember all of the details," Jeffries said. "But I do know that Miller clocked Boudreaux, really blindsided him, and Boudreaux just took him down. Somebody said after Boudreaux got him down on the ground, he stuck a knife right through the palm of Miller's hand."

"Really," Wyatt said.

"Thing was, he was cool as a cucumber when he did it, you know?" Jeffries took another drink of his watered down tea. "People said he didn't even seem like he was all that mad, just taking care of business, you know what I mean?"

"Yeah," Wyatt said, and glanced over at Maggie. She pretended not to notice.

"Mr. Jeffries, do you have any idea at all what was bothering Mr. Crawford around that time?" Maggie asked.

Jeffries shook his head. "Not really. He was having some financial problems, you know, putting a lot of money into that new building. The trouble with Boudreaux's father, but that was ongoing. So, I don't really know."

"What was his marriage like?" Maggie asked.

The man shrugged. "Good. They got married young, not too long after high school. We all went to school together, them and me and my wife." He shrugged again. "He loved the hell out of Beth. They were a good team."

"No problems?" Maggie asked.

"Of course they had problems. Everybody has problems. But they did okay." He pointed a finger at Maggie, like she'd transgressed in some way. "She never did get married again, you know, and she had chances. Plenty of good men would have stepped up."

Maggie nodded, and he seemed placated somewhat.

Several minutes and a few questions later, Maggie and Wyatt walked back out the front door. Maggie was glad to be outside, and Jeffries seemed equally glad that she was.

She and Wyatt walked to the driveway, and Maggie pulled her keys from her pocket. "What time is your doctor's appointment?" she asked Wyatt. Wyatt was due for his annual physical for work.

"Ten minutes," Wyatt said. "Where are you headed?"

"Carrabelle. Lana Burwell lives there now. She and her husband used to own Bayside Construction," Maggie said. "She finally got my message, and I'm heading over there to talk to her."

"Well, hopefully that'll be worthwhile."

"It only makes sense that somebody from there might have put Crawford in that wall," Maggie said.

"Yep, makes sense," Wyatt agreed. "Just remember that Fitch saw *two* guys with Crawford that night."

"Yeah, I know," she said. "That doesn't mean one of them was Boudreaux."

"Doesn't mean it wasn't," Wyatt said as he got into his cruiser.

CHAPTER

FOURTEEN

Bennett Boudreaux locked the door of his black Mercedes and walked from the sandy parking area on 13th Street onto the brick pavers that crisscrossed Lafayette Park.

Located not too many blocks from his home, Lafayette Park was a favorite with the locals. The large, white gazebo in the center of the park was a popular spot for family portraits, weddings and reunions. Neighborhood mothers brought their small children to play in the sandbox while they waited beneath the shade trees with younger children in strollers.

The Lafayette Pier, which jutted out into the bay from the back of the park was also a favorite spot for local fishermen, and it was to the pier that Boudreaux headed.

The last time Boudreaux had been there was a few months back. He'd asked Maggie to meet him there to talk. He found that somewhat ironic today, but he wasn't really in the mood for irony.

The park was nearly empty, it being the middle of a weekday afternoon and, as Boudreaux stepped onto the six hundred-foot pier, he saw that his appointment was the only other person present.

The hard soles of Boudreaux's leather shoes thumped against the wood, and sea birds called to each other as they coasted on the decent breeze above the water. That breeze rustled through the tall, feathery grass on either side of the pier, and through Boudreaux's meticulously combed hair.

He brushed it back out of his eyes and into place as he stopped about midway down the pier and nodded at Gray Redmond, who leaned back against the rail, his hands gripping the wood on either side of him.

"Good afternoon, Gray," Boudreaux said.

"Afternoon," Gray said, nodding slightly.

"What can I do for you?"

Gray looked down at the floor of the pier for a moment before answering. He looked Boudreaux in the eye when he did.

"This Holden Crawford thing," Gray said. "It's presenting problems."

"For whom?"

"For all of us, wouldn't you say?" Gray answered.

Boudreaux studied the other man for a moment. He had a good deal of respect for Gray. Gray had done something most eighteen year-old men couldn't do, and he'd done it well. He'd also done an admirable job of keeping it to himself.

"I'll admit it's inconvenient," Boudreaux said. "Particularly given the fact that Maggie is the one investigating the case. But it would have been inconvenient with anyone looking into it. It doesn't really change anything."

"It does if they're mainly looking at you," Gray answered.

"There's no evidence that I had anything at all to do with what happened to Crawford," Boudreaux said.

"You're still the main suspect, according to Maggie."

Boudreaux gently tapped at his left eyebrow for a moment as he studied Redmond's face.

"Maggie doesn't think I did it," he said finally. He saw Gray swallow, saw his eyes narrow just slightly.

"It doesn't matter what Maggie thinks, though, does it?" Gray asked. "She's not the only one working this case."

"I assume you're speaking of Sheriff Hamilton," Boudreaux said. Gray nodded just once. "Of course, he'd love nothing more than to see me convicted of something, but he's a straight arrow. He'll look for actual evidence, which he won't find."

"Right now, he's looking at your lack of an alibi," Gray said. "I should think it would serve your interests, legal and otherwise, to give it to him."

"I disagree. I don't think it would be in anyone's best interest," Boudreaux said. "We agreed, together, how we would handle this situation."

"That was thirty-eight years ago," Gray said.

Boudreaux could feel himself becoming frustrated. He didn't like it when done things came undone, and he preferred to never make decisions based on urgency.

"Maggie's bothered by this alibi thing," Gray said. "She's looking into it, whether she thinks you're involved or not."

"She won't find anything," Boudreaux said calmly.

"And why is that?"

"It's not there," Boudreaux answered. "Sheriff Bradford never put it on record."

"Why do you know that?" Gray asked.

Bellows had been an investigator for the Sheriff's Office for many years. It was widely suspected—accurately so—that he was also on Boudreaux's payroll. He was now comfortably settled in Vero Beach, retired on monies he'd earned from his sideline.

"I asked Gordon get rid of anything about it in Crawford's file," Boudreaux said. "The year Maggie joined the Sheriff's Office, actually. I thought it prudent. There was nothing there."

Gray stared past Boudreaux without expression. Boudreaux knew he was probably working that out in his head. It shouldn't take long.

Gray heaved a frustrated sigh and looked out at the end of the pier, where a pelican sat waiting for providence. After a moment, he looked back at Boudreaux.

"There's an ethical issue here," he said. "Regardless of what we agreed on back then, I could never in good conscience just stand by while you were arrested for something you didn't do."

He stopped and squinted out at the water, and Boudreaux saw the muscles of his jaw tighten and release.

"Regardless of how I feel about it, she wouldn't want it, either," Gray said to the bay.

"There's no reason to do anything we'll probably regret," Boudreaux said.

Gray looked back at him. "The truth is going to come out sooner or later," he said.

"Not until one of us tells it," Boudreaux said.

⚓ ⚓ ⚓

Maggie turned left from Maple Street onto Avenue B and gently braked as she waited for a squirrel to make up its mind about which side of the street it needed to be on. It was warm in the Jeep, and she rolled down her front windows before she moved on.

As Lafayette Park came up on her right, Maggie glanced over and saw her father's old Chevy pickup. Lafayette Picr was one of her father's favorite places to fish; he and Maggie had fished here many times while she was growing up, and now he often brought her kids here as well.

She parked next to the truck and got out. She had a little bit before she was due at Mrs. Burwell's, and maybe Daddy had something she could fix for dinner after.

She walked across the grass and onto the brick pathway that led to and around the gazebo, and then to the pier. She had just reached the near side of the gazebo when she looked out at the pier and saw her father.

Maggie stopped and stared.

She'd seen her father and Bennett Boudreaux together many times in her life. All of them had been at Sea-Fair, all of them had been as her father was getting paid for his day's harvest. Seeing the two of them out there on the pier, standing close together and obviously deep in conversation, was completely foreign to Maggie, and it took a moment for her to be sure she was actually seeing it.

Daddy wasn't wearing fishing clothes, nor was he holding a pole. Boudreaux didn't appear to be engaged in fishing, either. They appeared to be very engaged with each other.

Just that summer, Maggie had met Boudreaux on this same pier, at his request. Had he asked her father to do the same? She couldn't think of a single reason why he should. Her father didn't even sell his oysters to Sea-Fair anymore; he only worked part-time, and he sold small quantities at the farmer's market and sometimes directly to friends and neighbors.

Maggie's first instinct was to walk on out there and ask them what the hell they were doing, but the incongruity of it held her back. She couldn't think of one good reason for them to be there. She couldn't think of any bad ones, either, but given her father's feelings toward Boudreaux she couldn't help sensing that there was one.

She hesitated for a moment longer, then turned around and quickly walked back the way she'd come. She told herself it was because she should ask her father in private, and brushed away the thought that she just couldn't think of an answer she'd want to hear.

⚓ ⚓ ⚓

Lana Burwell lived in a small pink cottage in the center of the almost too quaint little town of Carrabelle, half an hour east of Apalach.

The small front yard was filled with flowering plants and cutesy yard accessories; garden plaques, gnomes, tiny windmills and deer frozen mid-step were everywhere. Maggie wasn't sure how Mrs. Burwell managed to make it around her yard to maintain all of her plants, but they looked robust enough.

Mrs. Burwell was fairly robust herself. She looked younger than Maggie knew she was, in that way that heavy people often do, and her voice was surprisingly high and dainty.

She invited Maggie inside, offered her coffee, which Maggie politely declined, then led her to a back room that looked to be part sewing room and part storage closet. The small sewing table was surrounded by boxes and totes that rose to the ceiling in places.

"After we talked, I went through a bunch of stuff, looking for payroll records and whatnot," the woman said as they picked their way through the room. "I'm afraid I didn't find any."

Maggie sidestepped a small pile of papers. "I'm sorry to hear that," she said.

"Well, it was so long ago, of course," Mrs. Burwell said. "Everything was paper then, not on computers like it is now. You run out of room, you throw stuff out."

"I don't suppose there's any chance you remember anyone who was working for you in 1977?" Maggie asked.

"Oh, goodness no. I don't remember what I did day before yesterday," Mrs. Burwell said. "And I wasn't too involved in the business, anyway. I was home raising four kids."

She stopped at one of several open boxes and tapped at the pile of yellowed manila folders and dark green hanging files on top. "I did find some tax returns, but they don't have employee names on them or anything, so not much help to you there. However, I did come across a bunch of awards and things we used to have hanging in the office, you know, licenses and civic awards and things, and that was when I remembered the Neighborhood League."

Mrs. Burwell was looking at Maggie happily, as though Maggie would understand the significance. She didn't.

"The Neighborhood League?"

"Yes! It doesn't exist anymore, of course, but we were very involved," Mrs. Burwell answered.

"What was it?"

"It was kind of a historic preservation thing," the woman said. "There were a few businesses involved. Like Goodwin's Hardware. They donated a lot of lumber and paint and things. We usually talked most of our guys into donating some labor."

Mrs. Burwell squeezed her way past a few more boxes to get to her sewing table. "Anyway, we always had a barbecue or picnic or something of that sort when that year's project was finished, and we had pictures from every single year hanging up in the front office. Good public relations, you know."

She put a hand on an open cardboard box on the sewing table. "Anyhoo, I was just starting to go through this when you knocked," she said.

Maggie stepped a bit closer and rose up on her toes as the older woman opened the flaps of the box. It was filled with pictures in cheap black frames. There was a stack of frames already on the sewing table, all of them coated with a thin veil of dust.

Mrs. Burwell started flipping through the pictures still inside the box. "I wish we'd boxed these up in some kind of order, but who knew we'd actually need to find one?" she said. "This is eighty-two. Here's eighty-seven. I don't even remember what the project was in seventy-seven. That may have been the year we worked on The Soda Shoppe. Nope, here it is!"

She pulled a frame out of the stack and held it up proudly. "It was the Fennimore House. They made it a bed and breakfast for a while."

Maggie was too far away to see much. She could make out the caption under the photo: "Fennimore

House Restoration – 1977." The picture itself was a faded black and white of a group of men sitting at a picnic table on the grass. Beyond them was the front of an imposing white Victorian home.

Maggie made her way closer as the woman wiped at the picture with one sleeve of her flowered blouse and peered at it.

"Of course, this won't have everyone who worked with us that year," she said. "We always had a lot of shrimpers and oystermen working with us on and off, too. But most of the guys will be here."

Maggie looked over the woman's shoulder as she tapped a bright pink nail on one or another face. "This is Frank Grasso. He passed away some years ago, poor guy. I don't know who this is. Here's the Swift boy… Chris or Craig, something like that. Very sweet."

Maggie maneuvered herself so that she could get a better look at the picture. There were more than a dozen men at the table, some looking at the camera, some not.

"I don't know him. Or him. This is my husband, of course." Mrs. Burwell let out a surprisingly delicate sneeze. "Goodness. Oh, this is Sam Richards, we actually became very good friends with him and his wife over the years. They live in Costa Rica now."

Maggie knew some of the surnames, but not all. She also recognized Harry Fox before Mrs. Burwell named him. Harry had been David's baseball coach in junior high.

"Oh, this is Paul McNamara," Mrs. Burwell said. "I forgot all about him."

She moved her finger, and Maggie suddenly felt weightless. She stopped breathing, and the sound of Mrs. Burwell's fingernail tapping on the lean, young face was the only sound in the room for a moment.

"Hm," the woman said. "Sorry, I don't know who that is."

Maggie did. It was her father.

CHAPTER

FIFTEEN

Maggie pulled in behind Wyatt's truck, and walked to the front door. When Wyatt opened it, he was barefoot, wearing his reading glasses and a worn pair of jeans.

"Hey," he said, sounding somewhat surprised.

"Hey," Maggie said. "Can I come in?"

"No, dumbass, of course not," he said as he opened the door wide.

Maggie went inside and, once Wyatt had closed the door, she distractedly let herself be hugged.

"Okay, what's up?" he asked.

Maggie sighed. "Do you have any wine?"

Wyatt frowned at her for a moment. "Yeah, come on."

Maggie followed him through the living room and to the kitchen, where she set her purse on the breakfast bar. The French doors from the dining area to the back patio were open, and the white sheers billowed a little in the breeze. The wind had died down quite a bit after the sun had set, but the air still had a touch of autumn to it.

Wyatt poured two glasses of red wine. "Tell me what's going on," he said.

Maggie took a healthy swallow, then put down the glass and pulled the picture from her purse. Mrs. Burwell had taken it out of the frame for her, and drawn little arrows between faces and names that she knew.

"What's that?" Wyatt asked.

"It's most of the guys who worked for Bayside Construction the summer of '77." Maggie placed the picture on the breakfast bar, upside down so that Wyatt could look at it.

"Okay," he said, tilting his head up a bit to see through his glasses.

Maggie took a breath and hesitated for a moment, reluctant to point out her father, like it might make him more "there" than he already was. Finally, she put one finger next to her father's face.

Wyatt bent a bit closer to the photograph, then finally stood back up.

"Maggie, this doesn't mean anything," he said quietly.

"But why didn't he mention it to me?"

"Why should he?"

"We were talking about the case," she answered. "Why wouldn't he tell me that he'd worked on the building where Crawford's body was found?"

"Okay, let's step back a second," Wyatt said, putting his hands on the counter. "This was almost forty years ago. He may have forgotten he even worked with Bayside."

"You don't think hearing about Crawford's body would jog his memory? Besides, my father doesn't forget much."

"Maggie, what's your point? Really?" Wyatt asked. "Because we both know your Dad."

"I'm not sure what my point is," she answered. "But I'm upset."

"Why? Almost every oysterman I know works other jobs to make ends meet. This is a small town. It's not that big of a coincidence that he happened to work for Bayside."

"No, it isn't," Maggie. "And it wouldn't bother me a bit if he had told me that."

She took another swallow of wine and willed it to take the edge off her nerves.

"I can see being surprised by this," Wyatt said as he tapped the picture. "But honestly, I don't see the big deal. Think about it. Do you really have any reason to think this means anything bad?"

Maggie looked up at him for a moment, then sighed. "Maybe."

"Like what?"

She chewed at the corner of her lip and stared at the counter. "I saw him talking with Boudreaux today, out on Lafayette Pier."

Wyatt pursed his lips a moment, his formidable moustache brushing at the bottom of his nose. "Okay. That's kind of surprising. But Maggie, they could have just run into each other. Gray goes fishing there all the time."

"Daddy wasn't fishing," she said. "And Boudreaux doesn't run into people."

Wyatt took off his glasses and sighed. "They did business together for years."

"At Boudreaux's place of business," Maggie said. "And not anymore."

Wyatt put his glasses down and took a drink of wine, waited.

"The last time I saw Boudreaux on that pier was over the summer. He asked me to meet him there," she said finally. "We talked about the rape, and Sport Wilmette."

"So…what?" Wyatt asked. "You think Boudreaux summoned your dad? For what reason?"

Maggie shook her head and shrugged, frustrated and tired of thinking. "I don't know. It just feels wrong, especially after seeing this picture."

"Look at me," Wyatt said, and put his hands on her shoulders. "Just ask him."

"No."

"Why not?"

"Because I don't question my dad," she said. "I don't interview my father."

"I'm not saying you should grill him. There's no reason to," Wyatt said. "But for your own piece of mind, just ask him about it."

Maggie sighed and took another drink of her wine. "Maybe. Eventually."

"Are you investigating this case or not?" Wyatt asked, a little sharply.

"Yeah, I am," she shot back.

"And we're trying to ID these guys in the picture so we can maybe find out if one of them bricked up Crawford, are we not?"

"Yeah," Maggie answered, less forcefully. "We are."

"None of whom was your father, and my Scrabble nemesis," Wyatt continued. "But we're still working the damn picture."

"Yeah."

"Now, what are you doing for dinner?"

Maggie took a second to change gears. "Going home to the kids and ordering pizza, because I suck at mothering and copping simultaneously."

"Why don't I order the pizza, and you go get the kids and bring them here?" Wyatt asked.

"I guess I could do that," she said.

"Kids and dogs only," Wyatt said. "No poultry."

⚓ ⚓ ⚓

Late the next morning, Wyatt walked into Maggie's office, a legal pad in one hand and a Mountain Dew in the other.

"Hey," he said as he came in.

Maggie looked up from her computer. "Hey."

She spun around to face him as he threw himself into the metal folding chair and took a swallow of his soda.

"So, found one more," he said, looking at his pad. "Craig Swift is an engineer in Atlanta now, God bless him. He worked for Bayside that summer, but he went back to college early—Georgia Tech—did a half term to make up some class. He was gone from here in early July."

"Okay," Maggie said. "Did he remember anyone from back then?"

"Just Burwell and Harry Fox," Wyatt answered. "He only worked for them during school breaks, and he wasn't from here. Sam Richards, the guy that lives in Costa Rica now? He was good friends with Craig's dad and got him a job with Bayside during school breaks. That summer was his last one, though."

"Why?"

"He graduated. Summa cum laude."

"Okay, so probably nothing there."

"Probably not," Wyatt agreed. "How are you coming along?"

"Two more IDs. Carol recognized this guy here on the end," she said, pointing at the picture on her desk. "That's Danny Grady."

"Rings a bell," Wyatt said.

"He's still local," Maggie said. "A shrimper. I left a message with his wife."

"Who else did you get?"

"This guy here," Maggie said. "This is Dwight's uncle, Howard Shultz. I remember him. He died about eight years ago."

"What did Dwight have to say about him?" Dwight Shultz was a deputy, a high-strung but completely upstanding young man that they often referred to as Dudley Do-Right.

"Nothing important, except that Howard wouldn't have been here mid-August," Maggie answered. "He got drunk on the Fourth of July and signed up for the Army. He was gone within a couple of weeks."

"Okay, so nada."

"Right," Maggie said.

"At least we're eliminating some people," Wyatt said.

He took a swig of his Dew and leaned over to peer at the picture.

"So, how many unknowns do we have left?" he asked.

"Four," Maggie answered.

Wyatt stared across the desk at her. When she failed to respond, he raised his eyebrows pretty much to his hairline.

"Alright, get off my back," Maggie said, standing up.

He took a drink and watched Maggie as she snatched up the picture, grabbed her purse from its hook, and started out.

"Tell him I'm gonna kick his elderly ass next Scrabble night."

"No. He only has one lung," Maggie said. "I don't think he can take that big a funny."

Wyatt frowned at her back as she left the office, then looked back at his legal pad. "Kick your ass, too," he said, to no one specific.

M aggie called her parents' house and learned that her father was cleaning the skiff, so she headed over to Scipio Creek Marina, just a few doors down from Boudreaux's place and the building where Crawford had last been seen.

When Maggie hit the docks, she saw that Daddy was hosing down the decks. He looked up when she got to his slip.

"Hey, Sunshine," he said.

"Hey, Daddy," Maggie said, squinting at him in the brutal sunlight. She'd left her sunglasses in the Jeep.

"What brings you over here?" he asked.

"I thought maybe you could help me with something," she said.

"Sure. What do you need?"

Maggie nervously pulled the photograph out of her purse. "I was wondering if you could take a look at this."

Gray shut the hose off, dried his hands on his work pants, and walked over to the rail. "Hop aboard."

He handed her onto the deck, then took the picture from her. Maggie watched his face, which went from mildly interested, to surprised, to blank within just a few seconds.

"Well," was all he said.

"I didn't know you worked for Bayside," Maggie said, trying for a casual tone.

He looked up at her. "Yes, I did. Not on a regular basis, but whenever things were slow," he said. "I was trying to save up some money for when your Mama and I got married."

Maggie had several questions she wanted to ask but, standing right there in front of her father, she couldn't bring herself to ask them. "Do you remember any of those guys with the question marks by their heads?" she asked instead.

"Let's see," Gray said, pulling the picture closer to his face. "This one here is Ray Dougherty," he said. "Remember him? He used to come over now and then."

Maggie looked at the face. "No, I don't remember him."

"He died in a car wreck...oh, back around '86 or '87," Gray said. "On his way to pick up some family from the airport in Tallahassee."

"That's too bad," Maggie said.

"So what's your interest in these guys?" Gray asked.

Maggie chewed at her lip. "Well, Bayside was doing the renovations on the building where Crawford was found," she said.

Gray studied Maggie's face for a moment. "That's right," he said finally. "I'd forgotten about that."

She didn't say anything, and Gray looked back down at the picture. "This guy here, holding up his beer, that's Terry Luedtke."

Maggie leaned over to look. Luedtke was standing up behind her father, and had raised his bottle to the camera. He looked to be in his early thirties. Maybe he'd still be around.

"Who is he?" Maggie asked. "I don't recognize the name."

"He was a nice guy," Gray said. "Give you the shirt off his back. He moved away after Crawford's closed."

"Why?" Maggie asked.

"Well, he worked for Crawford," Gray answered. "He was a processor. He took over as manager sometime after Crawford disappeared, then he left when Boudreaux closed the place. I'm not sure why. Maybe he just didn't want to work for Boudreaux."

Maggie thought about that for a moment. "What happened to the people that worked at Crawford's back then?"

"Most of them went to work for Boudreaux," Gray said. "I'll give him that at least; he didn't fire anybody."

Maggie looked at her father's face as he studied the picture in his hands. His longish hair had dropped over his brow, as it tended to do, and she wanted to brush it out of his eyes, as she tended to want. She also wanted to not ask or think anything that would ever hurt this man who would crawl through fire for her with only half a reason.

"Do you recognize any of these other guys we don't have names for?" she asked finally.

Gray tapped the picture with one finger. "This man, his name is right on the tip of my tongue, but I just can't get to it," he said. "I didn't know him very well."

"Can you think of anyone who's not in the picture that worked for Bayside back then?"

Gray ran a tongue along his lower lip. "I don't think so. But I was only there off and on, like I said, whenever I had time to make some extra money." He looked up at Maggie. "Your Grandpa's old boat was ailing pretty badly back then. This job helped me pay for a rebuilt engine."

Maggie nodded and took a breath before speaking. "Do you remember if there was a brick wall splitting up the flower shop, Daddy?"

Gray looked at her a moment. She thought maybe he was going to ask her a question, and she held her breath just a little. But then he shook his head. "I couldn't say. I didn't work on that building."

Maggie hadn't expected that answer. "You didn't?"

"No," he said. "They didn't need me over there yet. I just did trim work. Carpentry and so on. Cabinets. That kind of thing."

Maggie looked down the docks, pretending to be distracted by an outgoing shrimp boat.

"I just figured you would have," she said.

"No." Gray said. "And it was almost a year before anybody started back on that place. By that time I wasn't working for Bayside anymore."

"Why not?" Maggie asked.

"Because you came along," he said. "I didn't have time for side jobs anymore."

Maggie nodded again. "Gotcha," she said.

She smiled up at her father, squinting against the sun.

"Well, thanks, Daddy," she said. "I appreciate the help."

"No problem, Sunshine," Gray said.

He kissed her on the forehead, and she jumped back onto the dock and headed back to her car.

She would have been more relieved than she could remember being, if it weren't for the squirming sensation deep in her gut, telling her that Daddy had told her some of the truth, but not all of it.

⚓   ⚓   ⚓

The following afternoon, Maggie threw her pen down on her desk and rolled her head to get the kinks out of her neck.

The thick folder containing the missing persons file from 1977 lay open on her desk. Next to it was the much thinner file from the murder investigation. They'd had a lot more people to interview thirty-eight years ago.

Maggie stood up and arched her back, then grabbed her empty coffee mug and headed down the hall to the break room. She was trying to make the horrific office coffee into something worth drinking when Deputy Dwight Shultz walked by.

Dwight was thin, prematurely balding, and always seemed to be nervous, even when he was calm. Maggie adored Dwight, and worked hard at not thinking of Don Knotts every time she saw him.

"Oh hey, Maggie, there you are," Dwight said as he veered into the break room.

"Hey, Dwight," Maggie said, stirring one more sugar into her coffee.

"That guy William Overton called for you," he said, holding up a piece of scrap paper. "You know, the florist?"

"Yeah," Maggie said. "What did he need?"

"He said to tell you he put five suspicious bricks outside his back door for you," Dwight said.

Maggie squinted at Dwight. "What does he suspect these bricks of doing?" she asked.

"Well, uh, he suspects them of being tainted," Dwight said. "He says they have spots. He wants you to take 'em away."

Maggie sighed. "I'll stop by there later and throw them in his dumpster."

"He, uh, he was kindly agitated," Dwight said seriously.

"I'm sure he was," Maggie said. She took the paper from his hand. "Thanks, Dwight, I'll take care of it," she said.

"No problem."

They went in opposite directions once they left the break room. Dwight headed back to the main room up front, and Maggie headed for Wyatt's office. She nearly bumped into him coming out of it.

"Hey, I was just coming to talk to you," Wyatt said.

"Me, too," she said.

"Apparently," Wyatt said, walking back into his office.

Maggie followed him over to his desk. He sat down behind it, and she settled into one of the hideous red vinyl chairs in front of it.

"I've been going over the statements from '77," Wyatt said. "Interesting thing about Jeffries."

"Who?"

"Vincent Jeffries, Crawford's best friend," Wyatt answered.

"Oh, right," Maggie said. All of the names from almost four decades ago were starting to run together in her head. "What about him?"

"Well, his alibi may or may not be crap," Wyatt said.

"Why?"

Wyatt flipped through the pages he'd copied from the original file. "*Kojak* was on that night, I checked," he said.

"Nice," Maggie said, taking a regrettable sip of her coffee.

"Wikipedia," Wyatt told her. "However, according to his wife's statement, she was asleep when Jeffries came home that night. She worked late the night before—she was a nurse—and she was tired that night, which is why she didn't go out to this raw bar crawl thingy." Wyatt pushed his glasses up the bridge of his nose. "She woke up around eleven to find him watching TV out in the living room."

"Okay. So maybe he doesn't have that great an alibi," Maggie said. "Fitch saw Crawford and the other guys around ten."

"Right," Wyatt replied. "Conceivable that he could have been one of them."

"Why?" Maggie asked.

"Who knows? He seemed to think a lot of Mrs. Crawford. Maybe he had a thing for her."

"Maybe. But have you seen the pictures of her from back then?" Maggie asked.

"Yes, and she was very pretty."

"Very. And did you see Jeffries' wedding picture in the china cabinet?"

"No, I did not," Wyatt answered.

"He wasn't," Maggie said. "Pretty."

"Neither was Crawford," Wyatt countered.

"He wasn't bad looking," Maggie said.

"Are you gonna tell me now that only a good-looking guy could have done it?"

"No, wiseass, I'm saying that if Jeffries killed Crawford because he had a thing for his wife, then he was probably deluded."

"Whatever," Wyatt said. "It's a possibility."

"A possibility," Maggi agreed. "But then what about the other guy that was there?"

"I still think Boudreaux."

Maggie let out something that was half sigh and half grunt. "Boudreaux couldn't have cared less about some other guy's unrequited love," she said. "He sure as heck wouldn't kill over it."

"No, but he could have done it for his reasons, and Jeffries could have helped him for his," Wyatt said. "Boudreaux was the short guy and Jeffries was the taller one."

Maggie twisted her mug around in her hand for a moment, staring at the Sheriff's Office insignia as it went by.

"It doesn't feel right," Maggie said. "Meanwhile, while you were trying to find some way to fit Boudreaux into your theory, I heard back from Bay County on Terry Luedtke."

"The manager guy," Wyatt said.

"Yeah," Maggie said. "And my thing is more interesting than your interesting thing."

"And what is your thing?' Wyatt asked.

"This guy Luedtke took over as manager at Crawford's not too long after Crawford went missing," Maggie said. "Possible motivation."

"Possible," Wyatt said, but he didn't look enthusiastic about it.

"Then he moved to Lynn Haven in 1984, pretty much right after Boudreaux bought Crawford's business."

"Okay. But you said Gray told you that Boudreaux didn't fire anybody from Crawford's, so he moved for some other reason maybe."

"Maybe," Maggie said. "But he killed himself three months after he moved."

"Huh," Wyatt said, his face blank. He at back in his chair, took off his cap and ran a hand through his hair before he put his hat back on. "Okay, so maybe Boudreaux promised him a better job for helping him off Crawford, and didn't follow through. Or maybe the guilt was too much for this guy."

"I think you're painting yourself into corners trying to fit Boudreaux in," Maggie said. "You told *me* to keep an open mind."

"Not so open that everything falls out," Wyatt said. "And may I remind you that Boudreaux was already the main suspect; I didn't just squeeze him in."

"I know that," Maggie said. "But he doesn't fit."

"Like hell," Wyatt said.

"Anyway," Maggie said. "I'm going to look into Luedtke some more, and I think we should ask Mrs. Crawford what she can tell us about him."

"Okay. We shall," Wyatt said. "But I can't do it today. I have a meeting with the bigwigs."

"This late in the day? What's up?" Maggie asked.

"Sheriffy stuff," Wyatt answered, shrugging. "Do you want to go talk to her alone or do you want to wait until tomorrow?"

Maggie got up from her chair. "I'll wait. I'm going to make some more calls and then go home. The kids deserve a real dinner."

Wyatt watched her as she made her way to the door. "I still think it's Boudreaux," he said.

"And I still think that people who lay their lives on the line deserve decent coffee. Why don't you ask the bigwigs about *that*?" Maggie said as she left.

CHAPTER

SEVENTEEN

T he next morning was clear and cool, cool enough to pass for autumn to those who longed for it. There was a fairly brisk breeze, and the hibiscus and holly bushes that lined the driveway at Sunset Bay were bending with it in an almost celebratory way.

They'd taken Wyatt's cruiser, and Wyatt had been uncharacteristically quiet as he drove. Maggie was unused to silence with Wyatt. Even on days they'd spent every waking hour together, they always seemed to have something to talk about, even if it was football.

"So how did your meeting with the bosses go?" she asked, mainly for something to say.

"About how you would expect," Wyatt said.

"What was it about?"

"When you're the Sheriff, you can know what it's about," Wyatt said, but she could hear him forcing the lightness. "Right now, I'm the Sheriff, so I get to keep it to myself."

Maggie stared at the side of his head for a moment. His mood bugged her, but pushing didn't seem like a good idea. "Well," she said, forcing her own light tone. "If it's a pay cut, I'll be the first one to punch you in the face."

"Don't forget your Barney step stool," he said as he parked.

"You're an idiot," she said.

"Probably," he said, and got out of the car.

⚓ ⚓ ⚓

The nurse's assistant on duty that day was a different one from the week before. Wyatt spoke with her for a moment to explain who they were and to assure her that they just had a few questions, and she allowed them to go to Mrs. Crawford's room unescorted.

Wyatt knocked on the door, and he and Maggie were both surprised that Mrs. Crawford herself opened it, even though they knew she wasn't exactly an invalid.

Mrs. Crawford seemed a little taken aback to see them there, but she remembered who they were, or at least what they were.

"Good afternoon, Sheriff," she said, smiling.

"Hello, Mrs. Crawford," Wyatt said. "I hope we're not disturbing you. We're just hoping you can help us with a few things."

"Of course not. Come on in," she said, and opened the door wider.

Wyatt let Maggie go ahead and, as she walked in, Maggie took note of the fact that Mrs. Crawford looked, as she had the first time they'd met, like she was getting ready to go out for the day.

She was wearing tailored gray trousers, a lavender blouse, and gray leather ballet flats. Apparently, they were never going to find *her* wandering around in slippers and a robe. Maggie had to give her credit for that, considering that she herself would have been more than happy to live out her final decades in bare feet and yoga pants.

Mrs. Crawford led them over to the same table where they'd sat the other day.

"I got a call this morning saying I could go ahead with funeral arrangements for Holden," Mrs. Crawford said as they got settled. She looked at Maggie. "It's funny. I never actually thought I would."

"Would what, Mrs. Crawford?" Maggie asked.

"Have a service for him," the woman answered. "We had a small ceremony when Holden was declared legally dead, you know, just a few friends at the house."

"I'm sure this must be difficult, Mrs. Crawford," Wyatt said.

"Yes. He finally gets a funeral." She dabbed at one corner of her eye with her pinky finger, then smiled weakly. "Only, most of our friends and family are dead." She shook her shoulders a bit, as though she were shaking away her mood. "Well, what can I do for you?"

"We wanted to ask you about a couple of things that have come up since we started investigating your husband's case," Wyatt said. "First, we spoke to Vincent Jeffries the other day. He said your husband had seemed to be under a lot of stress the week or so before he disappeared."

Wyatt paused. Mrs. Crawford was staring at him as though she was still waiting for him to speak.

"Do you remember Mr. Jeffries, Mrs. Crawford?" Wyatt asked.

"Well, of course I do," she answered, sounding slightly irritated. "I'm not *that* far gone."

"I'm sorry," Wyatt said. "Do you remember what your husband was worried or upset about?"

Mrs. Crawford dabbed at the corners of her mouth as though she were tidying up her mauve lipstick.

"I don't think he was under any special stress," she said. "They asked me things like that when he first went missing, you know. Was he upset about anything, was there any reason he would just leave, that kind of thing."

"But nothing in particular comes to mind?" Maggie asked.

The older woman sat and looked out the sliding glass doors at the sunshine and the flowering bushes, and became noticeably bothered. Her fingers brushed idly at hair that wasn't out of place, and her eyes darted around what parts of the outside, or inside, world she could see.

"You know, sometimes it seems like it was some-one else's life, and sometimes it's my life and it was just the day before yesterday," she said finally, still staring out at the yard.

Maggie and Wyatt waited for her to go on, ready to remind her of the question that had been asked.

She finally looked back at them. "Holden had a lot going on that week," she said. "He was worried about money, and spending a lot of time on getting the new building ready."

She smiled and flipped her hair back, or would have, if it hadn't been shellacked into place. "He was doing that for me, you know," she said. "He knew I loved all those old buildings, and he was trying to di-versify a little. He wanted to put a café in there next to my new shop, you see."

She smiled at Wyatt as he nodded, then turned her gaze on Maggie. "He loved me very much."

"I'm sure he did," Maggie said.

"Are you married, Georgia?"

That stunned Maggie for just a second. "Georgia's my mother," she said. "I'm *Maggie* Redmond."

"Oh, I know," Mrs. Crawford said with a dismis-sive wave. "You know what I mean."

"So nothing special comes to mind, anything that he might have been particularly stressed about?" Wy-att asked.

"Not really, no," Mrs. Crawford answered. "I mean, it was a crazy week. My sister was very ill at that time; she had breast cancer."

Maggie cut her eyes over to Wyatt, who was looking at the table. His wife Lily had died of breast cancer just over ten years before. It was the main reason he'd moved from Cocoa Beach to Apalach.

"So, the business was very busy, and we had cheerleading championships," Mrs. Crawford was saying. "My car had finally died for good and we were trying to figure out how to pay for a new one. Our roof was leaking because of a storm the weekend before. One of those stupid pines."

She sighed, her amethyst pendant sliding off of her lapel. "So, yes, it was a rough week, but we'd had rougher ones."

Wyatt looked over at Maggie and raised an eyebrow at her.

"Mrs. Crawford, we also wanted to ask you about Terry Luedtke," she said.

She watched as the woman pursed her lips a few times, the way someone does when they're starting to say something. But she didn't.

"Do you remember him?" Maggie asked.

"Well, yes, of course I do," the woman said, frustration in her voice. "Of course. What about him?"

"He worked for you and your husband?"

"Well, he worked for Holden, yes," Mrs. Crawford said. "Then of course I asked him to run the business for me when we—well, when we didn't know what else to do. Holden didn't come back."

"What was he like?" Wyatt asked.

"Oh. Well, he wasn't very bright, but he was a very hard worker," Mrs. Crawford said. "And he knew the oyster business."

"Why did he leave after Boudreaux bought you out?" Wyatt asked.

Mrs. Crawford stared at him for a moment, then nervously twisted a strand of hair that hung against her neck. "Well, he...I think it was partly that he didn't want a new boss. But he also...well, he had started having feelings for me, you know. He said he had feelings for me."

"And you didn't return those feelings?" Maggie asked.

"No."

"Was this something new, or had he been interested in you before your husband's disappearance?" Wyatt asked gently.

"Oh, I see what you're—but, no, I don't think he did." She let go of her hair and fiddled with her necklace instead. "But you have to understand, he was a very sweet guy. He wouldn't have hurt a fly, I don't think."

"Did you stay in touch with him after he moved away?" Maggie asked.

"No," Mrs. Crawford answered. "It would have been uncomfortable."

Wyatt leaned forward, folded his hands on the table. "Mrs. Crawford, did you know that he committed suicide just a few months after he left Apalach?"

Mrs. Crawford stared at him a moment, then put a finger to her lips. "No. I don't think I knew that," she said.

She shook her head as though to clear her thoughts, then looked over at Maggie.

"Oh, honey," she said. "Georgia, I taught you better than that."

"I'm sorry?" Maggie said.

Mrs. Crawford reached over and grabbed the clip from the back of Maggie's head. "You have such beautiful hair, too beautiful to walk around like that."

Maggie's dark hair fell down around her shoulders, and Mrs. Crawford fluffed at the ends a little. Her fingertips were cold and dry against Maggie's neck, and Maggie barely suppressed a shiver.

"That's much better," Mrs. Crawford said. "Although I still say if you get a few layers put in, you'll look so much better. You know, something like Jaclyn Smith."

Mrs. Crawford stood up and pulled a few bobby pins out of her pants pocket. Maggie tried to cringe without cringing as the woman stood behind her and started gathering her hair up.

"Just remember, no matter where you go, or what kind of day you're having, it's still important to look your very best," the woman said.

Maggie looked at Wyatt. He was trying to keep his face neutral, but she could see the sadness there, though she wasn't sure which of them he felt worse for.

Mrs. Crawford finished fashioning Maggie's hair into a proper bun, and her fingertips brushed the sides of Maggie's face as she pulled out a few select tendrils.

"Oh, yes, so much better," she said as she sat back down. "It always pays for a girl to make just a little extra effort."

She patted Maggie gently on the cheek, and Maggie felt an odd mix of sympathy and revulsion.

"Just ask Gray," the old woman said, and gave Maggie a wink.

CHAPTER

EIGHTEEN

Maggie took a deep breath of dementia free air the moment she and Wyatt stepped back out onto the brick pathway.

"That was uncomfortable," Wyatt said.

"If you ever again just sit there and let somebody do my hair, I'll kick you in the head," Maggie said.

"I don't see how it could come up again," Wyatt said. "It does look nice, though."

Maggie rolled her eyes, but Wyatt pretended not to notice as he looked over at the main building.

"I want to see who's on Mrs. Crawford's visitors list," he said.

"What are you looking for?" Maggie asked.

"Anybody," Wyatt answered. "She says there's no one to come to the funeral, but she was a popular woman. Everybody can't be dead."

"I don't know. She seems like she's very hung up on appearances," Maggie said. "Maybe she didn't tell anyone she was coming here."

"It's not that easy to just drop off the face of the earth," Wyatt said.

"It is if you're not on Facebook."

Wyatt gave her a look that said she'd scored that point. "Let's go check."

"You go," Maggie said. "I want fresh air. That woman made me feel like a ghost."

"OK, I'll meet you back at the car," Wyatt said.

Maggie watched him head down the path that led to the main building, then she started on the one that led through a pleasant, parklike area and ended up at the parking lot.

She was halfway to the parking area when something caught her eye to the left, and she saw a man sitting on a bench, facing a small, manmade pond with a fountain in the center. It was Evan Caldwell.

Maggie stopped for a moment, unsure if she should disturb him, then headed across the grass.

"Mr. Caldwell," she said when she arrived at the bench.

He looked up, a cigarette in one hand and a Coke can in the other. The lip of the can was edged with ashes. There were dark shadows beneath Evan's eyes, but he gave her something of a smile.

"Maggie. How are you?" He scooted over a bit, though it wasn't necessary, and waved his cigarette at the bench. She hesitated a moment, then sat beside him.

"I'm fine, thank you," she said. "How's your wife?"

"The same," he said quietly, then took the last drag of his cigarette. "She's always the same."

"Is she here for rehab?" Maggie asked.

Evan looked at her, his black hair riffling a little in the breeze. It needed a trim. He pulled another cigarette out of his shirt pocket and held it up. When Maggie shook her head, he lit it. He blew out some smoke before he answered, looking out at the pond.

"She's in a coma," he said.

Maggie felt a weight of sympathy settle into her chest. "I'm sorry," she said.

He looked at her and smiled half-heartedly. "I never know what to say when people say that," he said. "Me, too?"

He took another drag of his cigarette and shrugged one shoulder.

"I usually end up just saying 'thank you,' but I feel like I should apologize for making people uncomfortable."

"I'm not uncomfortable," Maggie said. "Just sorry."

"Thank you," he said, then smiled. "Are you here about your case?"

"Yes," Maggie answered.

"How's that going?"

"It's hard, trying to unroll a ball of string someone rolled up thirty-eight years ago," she said.

"I'll bet," he said. "Especially if you have a murder that was investigated as a missing persons case."

"Is that all you do? Missing persons?"

"No. But I seem to have a knack for finding people that everyone else has stopped looking for," he answered.

"What's your secret?"

"Hell if I know," he said. He looked over at her, then turned his head a bit so he wouldn't blow smoke in her face. "I'll tell you this, though. We tend to look for complicated scenarios. I blame the cop shows on television. We bypass the simple solutions, and look for something more clever, more interesting." He tapped the end of his cigarette over the grass. "Then after all the tail-chasing, we usually end up finding out that the simple answer was the right one all along. They didn't call Einstein Einstein for nothing."

Maggie nodded. "I think I'd have to agree with you," she said. "Only I'm not sure what the simple answer is in this case."

"Take away everything you think, and everything everyone else thinks—or thought back then—and pare it all down to only the naked, known facts. The absolute solids. Throw out half the eyewitness testimony if you have any. Then look at what you have left and you'll usually have the bare bones solution."

Maggie nodded again, and picked at a thread on the knee of her jeans.

"Any of your primaries still around? Besides the widow?" Evan asked.

"A few. The former Sheriff. The guy's best friend. A local who's a professional suspect." Maggie stopped there, leaving her father off the list.

"Well, watch your perception of those people," Evan said. "They may look frail and sweet with their Bingo markers and their funny hats, but don't make the mistake of discounting them because they're elderly. They weren't elderly then."

"Good point," Maggie said, and pictured her father at eighteen, Boudreaux at twenty-two. Mrs. Crawford at Maggie's own age.

Evan dropped his cigarette butt into the Coke can and stood up.

"I've got to get back inside," he said, holding out his free hand. Maggie shook it.

"Thank you for the advice," she said.

"Take it for what it's worth," he said, then gave her half a wave and started across the grass toward the main building.

Maggie watched him go, saw weariness and maybe defeat in the set of his shoulders, reluctance in his pace. The overactive nurturing response in her made her want to stock his fridge with casseroles and launder his bedding.

Wyatt was right: this place just plain sucked.

⚓   ⚓   ⚓

"In the four years she's been there, she's never had a visitor, other than her family doctor and her lawyer," Wyatt said as they headed out of Port St. Joe. "You don't think that's weird?"

"Sure I think it's weird," Maggie said. "I just don't know if it means anything."

"I'm still keeping it as a notable weirdness," Wyatt said.

They rode in silence for several minutes, and Maggie looked out the window at the pines and overgrown brush that lined that stretch of Hwy 98, a desolate length of road that Sky had once said would be a perfect location for *The Walking Dead*.

"I ran into Evan Caldwell in the main lobby," Wyatt said after a bit.

"Yeah, I was talking to him outside," Maggie said.

Wyatt was quiet for a moment. "She slipped and fell and hit her head on a dock," he said finally. "That's it."

"That's awful," Maggie said. "Was he there?"

"No, he was working," Wyatt answered. "All she did was hit her head." He sighed. "You just never know when life's going to jump out and bite you."

Maggie looked over at Wyatt's profile. The laugh lines around his mouth were deeper, tighter, and he looked straight ahead at the road. She knew he was thinking about his wife. He and Lily had been married fifteen years when she'd died, from a cancer she hadn't even told him she had until it was absolutely necessary.

Maggie couldn't think of anything to say that was appropriate but not pithy, so she said nothing at all.

"You're hung up on Luedtke," Wyatt said after a while.

"Yeah," Maggie said, grateful for the change of subject.

"She said he was harmless."

"She said I was my mother," Maggie said. "Besides, everybody always says that so-and-so was a nice guy, until they find out he buried his parents in the basement."

"I'll give you that the suicide thing is a bell-ringer," Wyatt said. "We need to see if we can find anyone that knew him pretty well."

"I've got Dwight looking into it," Maggie said.

"I still think Boudreaux," Wyatt said.

"I know." Maggie looked back out the window. "I don't."

"But your reasons are partly personal," Wyatt countered.

"So are yours," Maggie said.

"I won't argue that."

⚓ ⚓ ⚓

A couple of hours later, Maggie and Wyatt sat on opposite sides of her desk, comparing notes on their day.

"So, I ran down the nurse that helped take care of Mrs. Crawford's sister," Wyatt said. "Just to confirm what she told officers back in '77. Please thank me for keeping an open mind."

"Thank you," Maggie said dryly.

"She says yeah, Mrs. Crawford was there that night, got there around eight-thirty," Wyatt said. "According to her, and she's a very sweet lady who also says she's seen me in the paper and I'm a doll-baby—her words—according to her, Mrs. Crawford was there a lot at night. Sometimes she spent the night so someone was with her sister until the morning nurse came."

"She didn't have round the clock care? She died like two months later, didn't she?"

"Yeah, but no. A nurse came in the morning to fix her something to eat, help her bathe, give her meds, that kind of thing," Wyatt said. "Another nurse, usually Mrs. Porter, came in the evening to do it all over again, but she didn't have someone overnight. She was ambulatory and lucid, though."

"That's so sad," Maggie said.

"Yeah." Wyatt looked down at his notes. "We were lucky. We had hospice. Good hospice." He coughed into his hand. "Anyway, she says Mrs. Crawford was there when she left around nine."

"And where did the sister live again?"

"Off Gibson Road," Wyatt said.

"Okay."

"See, I'm keeping an open mind," Wyatt said.

"I'll get you a sticker," Maggie said.

Wyatt looked toward her open door. The hallway was empty.

"How about you come over for dinner instead?" he asked. "You said the kids had sleepovers tonight, right?"

"Yeah."

"Then you should come over," he said.

Maggie nodded. "Okay. Or you could come out to my house. I have actual food."

"You're a delight," Wyatt said. "But no. I'd like you to come over. Wear something nice."

"Why? And what are you saying?"

"I'm not saying anything. I just think it would be nice if you wore something without legs. I have a surprise for you."

"That sounds kind of suggestive," Maggie said.

"Quit being a letch," Wyatt said. "Are you coming?"

"Yeah," Maggie said, a bit snippily.

Wyatt opened his mouth, no doubt to shred her with some witty remark, but he was interrupted by Dwight appearing in her doorway.

"Oh, hey, y'all," Dwight said. "I finally got hold of that guy Luedtke's brother."

"What did he have to say?"

"Well, he says Luedtke got dumped," Dwight answered. "That's why he moved over there where his brother lives."

Maggie sat up a little straighter. "Who dumped him?"

"He didn't know. Luedtke wouldn't talk about it," Dwight answered. "But, hey, when they went through his things afterward, they found a ring. Looked like an engagement ring, the brother said. He ended up pawning it, which is kinda sad."

"Yeah," Maggie said. "Is he sure Luedtke never said who she was?"

"Yeah, real sure," Dwight answered. "Not a peep. Love, huh? It's a real kick in the pants."

"Yeah, it can do that to you," Wyatt said, almost under his breath.

"Anyhow, that's what I got," Dwight said. "You need anything else?"

"No, thanks, Dwight," Wyatt said.

Once Dwight had gone, Wyatt looked at Maggie.

"I'm telling you," he said. "Two men, two motivations, working together toward a common goal."

Maggie shook her head. "If Boudreaux wanted to kill Crawford, he'd just do it," she said. "He wouldn't have someone else there as a witness."

"Maybe he didn't even know Luedtke was there," Wyatt said. "Maybe Luedtke was working late and came out when he heard a ruckus."

"And?"

"And saw a chance for Mrs. Crawford to not be a missus, and helped Boudreaux get rid of the body," Wyatt said.

Maggie shook her head again. "Boudreaux would have just killed him."

"I thought your version of Boudreaux was a great guy," Wyatt said.

"I don't have my own version of Boudreaux," Maggie said.

"Sure you do," Wyatt said. "Why wouldn't you? But it's colored by gratitude."

Maggie almost replied that she'd kind of liked Boudreaux *before* he'd saved her life, but caught herself.

"Boudreaux has an alibi," she said instead.

"He says he doesn't," Wyatt countered.

"He's lying."

"Why?" Wyatt asked.

"I think he was with somebody important," she answered. She got a picture of her dad and Boudreaux on the pier, and pushed it out of her head. "Somebody it wouldn't be good to be with."

"Maggie, this was umptity-ump years ago," Wyatt said. "He wasn't pals with all these senators and congressmen back then."

"Still," Maggie said.

"I've got some stuff I need to do," Wyatt said as he stood up and stretched his back. "Six-thirty good?"

"Yeah, sure. No legs."

She watched Wyatt head down the hall, and then sat there tapping her pen on the edge of her desk. She sat there like that for several minutes, then flipped through her notes before picking up her phone and dialing.

Bradford Wilson answered on the second ring, but he didn't sound too excited when Maggie said who it was.

"What can I do for you, Lieutenant?" he asked.

"Boudreaux's alibi," she said.

"What about it?"

"He needs it."

"Then ask him," Wilson said.

"I have. He says he didn't have one," Maggie said. "You say he did."

Wilson was silent, though she could hear him breathing.

"It usually happens in the reverse, doesn't it?" Maggie asked.

"Look, I've told you everything I remember," Wilson said finally.

"You told me crap," Maggie answered, unable to keep the frustration out of her voice. "Both of you are lying, and you're telling opposing lies."

"I don't like your tone," Wilson said, trying and failing to sound authoritative.

"I don't like your ethics," Maggie said. "Wyatt is pretty convinced that Boudreaux was involved in Crawford's murder. I need to know whether or not he had an alibi and, if he did, what that alibi was."

"Why?"

"What do you mean, why? Because I don't think he did it."

"He didn't," Wilson said. "I told you that. Listen, I don't want any damn problems with Bennett Boudreaux."

"You remember that he didn't do it, but you don't remember who or what he said his alibi was?"

"He didn't, dammit," Wilson said.

"What does that mean?" Maggie asked.

"He said he was home alone," Wilson said, sounding like she was torturing him for answers.

"So why does the case file say he had an alibi?"

"Because his alibi came forward, dammit!"

Maggie sat there for a second. That wasn't one of the answers she'd expected.

"Who?" she asked.

"Look, lady," Wilson said. "Your grandfather meant a great deal to me. If I could help you I would. I can't. Subpoena me if the opportunity arises."

He hung up on her, and Maggie sat there with the phone to her ear for a moment, angry as hell with no one to yell at.

Then she stood up, shoved the phone in the back pocket of her jeans, grabbed the case file and her purse, and stalked out the door.

When Maggie stopped by Sea-Fair, Boudreaux's receptionist reluctantly told her that Boudreaux had just walked over to Boss Oyster, so that was where Maggie went. She could have called Boudreaux directly, but she really didn't feel like giving him a lot of time to think before they talked. Of course, he seemed to think very well with or without notice, but Maggie liked to believe she was giving herself some kind of advantage.

When Maggie walked into Boss, she could see through the picture windows that Boudreaux was sitting in his usual spot on the deck out back, the same spot where she had sat with him just a few months ago, familiarizing herself for the first time with his particular brand of verbal cat and mouse.

She waved off one of the servers, Beatrice, who was headed in her direction with a tray of dirty dishes, then walked on out back. Boudreaux was leaning back in his chair, watching a small black cat gnaw a fish head out on the dock. He held a sweating bottle of Red Stripe in his hand.

He glanced over as Maggie approached. "Maggie," he said with a surprised smile. Always the gentleman, he stood up, setting his beer down on the table.

"Mr. Boudreaux," Maggie said.

"Please, sit down," Boudreaux said. She did, and they considered each other across the table. "Are you here for a late lunch or an early dinner?"

"Neither," she answered. "I came to talk to you."

He smiled politely at her, and the skin around those startling blue eyes crinkled just a bit. "Well, it's always good to see you," he said.

Beatrice scurried over, her left arm lined with baskets of grouper sandwiches.

"Would you like something to drink?" Boudreaux asked.

"Just some tea, thanks," Maggie said to Beatrice.

"Sure thing. Back in a sec," the girl answered, and hurried over to two young couples seated a few tables away.

"You'll share my oysters, then" Boudreaux said.

"I'm really not hungry," Maggie replied.

"They're oysters," Boudreaux said back. "You don't have to be hungry. And a gentleman never eats in front of a lady."

Maggie sighed and looked out at the water. Boudreaux took a sip of his beer and sat back in his chair and waited.

Maggie didn't feel she would be violating anything by being frank with Boudreaux. She wasn't going to tell him anything he didn't already know. Even so, she felt just a twinge of guilt, like she was undermining Wyatt in some way.

She looked around to make sure that no one was within easy hearing before she spoke.

"Wyatt's pretty well convinced that you're in this somehow. The Crawford murder," Maggie said when she finally looked back at him.

Boudreaux didn't look even a little surprised by that. "I see," was all she got from him.

"This is an issue for me," Maggie continued, lowering her voice a bit. "Because I don't think you killed Crawford."

"Why is that, Maggie?" he asked quietly.

"Well, for one thing, you wouldn't have needed to stab him more than once."

Boudreaux smiled at her then. "No, I wouldn't," he said smoothly, raising his beer to her. "Thank you for what could be a compliment."

Maggie watched him as he took a drink of his beer.

"For another thing, you're right-handed," she said.

"Is that significant?" he asked after he'd swallowed.

"Significant enough," she answered.

She watched him watch her, irritated that he seemed to have an endless supply of patience when he was waiting for someone else to lay things out.

Beatrice arrived with Maggie's iced tea, and Maggie was grateful for something and someone else to focus on for a moment. She really didn't think the conversation was going to be very fruitful.

"Thank you," Maggie said, as Beatrice set her glass on a paper napkin.

"You're welcome," the girl said. "You having oysters or do you want your grouper chowder?"

"No, nothing, thanks," Maggie said. "This is fine."

"Okay, let me know if you change your mind," Beatrice said. "Your oysters will be out in just a sec, Mr. Boudreaux."

"Thank you," he said, still watching Maggie.

Maggie waited until Beatrice had walked away, then sighed at Boudreaux.

"Your alibi," she said.

"There's no such animal," he said.

"Mr. Boudreaux, something just came out of your mouth that I wouldn't hold in my bare hand," Maggie said.

Boudreaux didn't try very hard to hide a bit of a smile.

"Bradford Wilson says you had an alibi," Maggie said.

"What was it?" Boudreaux asked her smoothly.

"How would I know? It's not in the case file and he won't tell me, but Wyatt and I already told you that," Maggie said, and she was unable to keep the frustration out of her voice.

"Bradford Wilson was a moron," Boudreaux said.

"That's probably true, but he's not a schizophrenic, so I don't think he imagined it."

"Here you go," Beatrice announced cheerfully. Maggie sat back in her seat as Beatrice set down a metal tray with a dozen gorgeous raw oysters and handful of lemons.

"Thank you, Beatrice," Boudreaux said. "These are beautiful."

"You need another Red Stripe?" she asked him.

"No, thank you," he answered. "This is fine."

"Alrighty. Well, you enjoy those," Beatrice answered, and headed back inside.

Maggie looked out at the water, watched as a pelican did some hang gliding over the close end of Big Towhead Island.

"Here," she heard Boudreaux say.

She looked back at him. He was holding up an oyster.

"No, thank you," she said.

"Straight up, just like you like them," he said.

Maggie wanted to say something sharp and dismissive, but she'd been bred to be so flipping polite. And the oyster looked good, plump and glistening in its puddle of brine.

She sighed and took the oyster from him, her fingertips brushing against his as she did. "Thank you," she said.

He smiled at her, picked up another oyster from the tray and lifted it between them. "Bottoms up," he said, and they both slid their oysters into their mouths.

Maggie swallowed the salty juices, then bit into the sweet, tender flesh and chewed. She closed her eyes as she swallowed, and when she opened them, Boudreaux was working on his next one.

"Do you know why I love these so much?" he asked, as he placed precisely one drop of Tabasco on his oyster.

"Because they're amazing?"

"That, too," he answered. "But I started digging for crawfish and helping my father sort shrimp back when I was probably five or six years old. He started me out early. I worked for free, of course."

He took a slice of lemon and squeezed just a bit onto his oyster.

"I remember when I was about seven, I was in his first plant, learning how to pack oysters. They looked so good, and I was hungry. I'd been working all morning. So I popped one into my mouth, and my father showed up out of nowhere and slapped me in the back of the head, so hard I spit it right back out. He said to me, 'We don't ever eat the money, boy,' and I never did again, not around him."

He raised his shell to her. "Now I eat them sometimes three times a day."

He ate his oyster, then smiled at her. "Of course, I'm not whining that my bastard of a father—if you'll please overlook my language—made me the cold killer that people think I am, but he did contribute to my love of the oyster."

"Yes, I've heard that your father was a real winner," Maggie said.

"It takes a great deal of character to be a father," Boudreaux said. "Not all of us are qualified." He took a drink of his beer. "You've seen how well I did with my stepsons."

"I don't think I've ever met Craig," Maggie said, speaking of the younger of the two.

"He's seldom here," Boudreaux said. "Which has probably worked in his favor."

Maggie didn't respond, just watched him. Finally, he left the oysters alone and sat back in his chair. He regarded her for a moment.

"There is no alibi, Maggie," he said softly.

"That's bull, Mr. Boudreaux. Apparently your alibi came forward when you refused to give one."

Boudreaux's left eye twitched, almost imperceptibly, and Maggie regretted that last statement. She hadn't thought about repercussions to Bradford Wilson before she'd made it.

"There's a note in the case file," she lied. "But there's no name."

"Someone was less than thorough with the case file, then," he said.

"If whoever you were with was willing to come forward, why won't you just tell me?" Maggie asked. "This isn't a game. You're the primary suspect."

"You know that's not going to hold up, Maggie," Boudreaux said. "There's no evidence against me, for the very simple reason that I had nothing to do with this thing. I don't need an alibi."

"But why won't you give it?' Maggie asked.

Boudreaux set his beer aside and propped his elbows on the table, folded his hands.

"It's a matter of honor," he said, staring her in the eye. "And I happen to know that you believe in such a thing."

Maggie stared at him a moment. "Honor," she said flatly.

"That's correct."

Maggie took a deep breath and looked out at the dock. The little black cat was dragging his fish head toward the restaurant. Maggie gave herself a moment to rein in her anger by wondering how the heck any cat living at Boss could be so skinny.

When she looked back at Boudreaux, he was still sitting there with his chin on his hands, watching her.

"Why were you out on Lafayette Pier with my father?' she asked, before she knew she would ask it.

That did seem to surprise Boudreaux, but only for a second. He sat back in his chair and scratched at his eyebrow for a moment, but he never took his eyes from hers. She felt, as she often did, that he could see the exact color of her marrow with those eyes.

"Is this a change of subject, or is this somehow related to our current topic?" he asked her quietly.

"It's a question," she answered.

"I should think you'd ask him," Boudreaux said. "You're so close."

"Actually, it's easier to ask you hard questions."

"And I suppose this would be a hard question to ask," Boudreaux said. "Are you concerned that I'm trying to taint Gray in some way?"

"Actually, I had a hard time coming up with a reasonable explanation," Maggie said. "Given the way he feels about you."

Maggie was suddenly and inexplicably concerned that she'd hurt Boudreaux, and she hastened to add, "He worries about me...about the fact that you and I have something of a friendly relationship."

Boudreaux looked at her for a moment, almost sympathetically. "Yes, I'm sure he does," he said. "I offered him a position in my company. That's why we were talking."

"What? Why?"

"Why not? I've done business with Gray for years. He knows oysters and he's a man of integrity."

"Why were you talking on the pier?' Maggie asked. "That seems like a conversation for the office."

"Not if the person whose position I was offering still happens to work for me," Boudreaux said. "In any event, Gray said 'no.' He may have retired for health reasons, but it seems to suit him."

He sat up and handed her another oyster. She took it without thinking.

"He also thanked me for what happened during the hurricane," Boudreaux said, focused on squeezing some lemon onto his oyster.

Maggie watched him, and when he glanced up at her, she saw those eyes, cold, hard, enraged, over Dewitt Alessi's shoulder as Boudreaux pulled him off of her. She saw those eyes just inches from hers, as they both clung to a tree on her flooded property, and he confided to her that Miss Evangeline was the only woman he'd ever loved.

They had both been through an ordeal that day. She had almost been killed, and he had killed to prevent that. They were both seriously injured, and they'd taken turns rescuing each other, getting back to the safety of her house.

Their shared experience had created a certain intimacy that Maggie assumed would always be there, but it had only solidified something that had already been forming, something that had started the day she'd stood there underneath his mango trees, and told him his nephew Gregory was dead.

Maggie swallowed, but she didn't blink under Boudreaux's gaze.

"I would imagine that your alibi came forward as a matter of honor, too, Mr. Boudreaux," she said.

"I'm not sure what their reason was, Maggie," he said. "I'm only concerned with my own."

He handed her another oyster.

"Thank you," she said, after she'd swallowed it. "I need to go."

She stood, but he was standing before she was. He held out a hand and she took it. As refined as he was, his calloused hands reminded her of her father's.

"Try not to be too upset, Maggie," he said. "It'll work out the way it's supposed to."

"And how is that?" she asked.

"I don't know," he said, with an almost sad-looking smile. "Whichever way that is."

Maggie let go of his hand and turned and walked away. As was usually the case, she'd come away from a conversation with Boudreaux feeling like she had more questions than when she'd walked in.

⚓ ⚓ ⚓

Boudreaux watched Maggie walk away, watched the screen door slap shut behind her, and then he sat back down and took a long drink of his beer.

One insignificant night out of thousands. One careless, thoughtless act. Such an unimpressive beginning to what would probably be his undoing, one way or another.

Whell Maggie pulled into the driveway next to Wyatt's truck, he was standing by his hood, drinking a Mountain Dew. Maggie was surprised but somewhat flattered to see him wearing nice trousers, and a shirt that didn't have flowers or turtles all over it.

He straightened up and looked at her as she got out of her Jeep. "Well. Don't you look pretty," he said.

She felt herself turn a little red. To her mind, skirts and dresses were for church or weddings. The fact that she'd left the house in a skirt and blouse without a special occasion made her feel self-conscious and ungainly. It hadn't helped that Sky had ridiculed her relentlessly while she'd tried on sixteen different combinations.

"It's just Wyatt, Mom," she'd said. "At Wyatt's *house.* Could you spaz less?"

Maggie stood in front of Wyatt now, and was convinced that he knew exactly how many outfits she'd tried on. And that he thought she'd chosen the wrong one.

"Thank you," Maggie said anyway. "You look very nice."

He walked over to her and wrapped an arm around her waist, then kissed her forehead. "Hop in the car," he said as he turned away.

"What? Why?"

He tossed his Mountain Dew in the recycle can by the driveway and opened his door. "I told you. I have something to show you."

"What is it?' Maggie asked, as she opened the passenger door.

Wyatt waited until she'd gotten inside. "Do you have to know everything ahead of time?"

Maggie thought about that for a moment. "Yes."

"Too bad," he said, and started the truck.

"Where are we going?" she asked, as he pulled out onto the street.

"You'll see."

"Is it your intention to annoy me?"

"Usually, yes," he answered. "But this time it's just my intention for you to shut up and let things unfold."

"There are things that have to unfold?"

"You make it sound so threatening," he said, turning onto D Street.

Maggie noticed that he wasn't looking at her much, and that he even seemed a little nervous. Wyatt was normally so laid-back that he made potheads look anxious, so this concerned her just a bit.

"So you're not going to tell me anything?' she asked.

"No."

Maggie forced herself to ride in silence for a few minutes, until Wyatt turned left onto Market Street, made a wide U-turn, and parked in front of Up the Stairs, one of the few 'nice' restaurants in town.

She had her mouth open to ask him what they were doing, but he was already out of the truck. She started to get a sinking feeling in her stomach, and clutched her purse in her lap as he came around the truck and opened her door. If it weren't for the skirt, and for the shirt that was not Hawaiian, Maggie could have believed they were going across the street across the street for an ice cream cone at The Old Time Soda Fountain, which happened to be a favorite spot for Wyatt.

"Out you go," he said.

"Wyatt, what are you doing?"

"Waiting for you," he answered.

"What do you want to show me?"

"Well, right now I want to show you what it's like to disembark from a truck, Maggie," he said.

"First tell me what we're doing here," she said.

"You know you weigh less than a bag of squirrels, right?" he asked. "I can pick you up."

Maggie looked at Wyatt's face. It looked a lot more serious than his words. "You're scaring me," she said quietly.

"I'm not trying to scare you," he said gently. He held out a hand. "It'll be okay, Maggie. I promise."

Maggie took his hand and stepped down from the truck. He closed the door and pulled her to the sidewalk.

"Wyatt, we can't do this," she said as she tried to keep up with his much longer legs.

"Well, it's what we're doing."

"Wyatt, you'll lose your job."

"Maggie, half the people in this town already think we're sleeping together," he said as he opened the door for them.

"But we're not!"

"Really beside the point," he said.

Once they got upstairs, Maggie was too flustered to think of anything else she could say, particularly in front of other people who were waiting to be seated. Wyatt, apparently, had a reservation for two out on the balcony overlooking Market Street.

He held her hand the entire way as the hostess led them out there, and as she glanced around at a couple of familiar faces, Maggie couldn't help feeling like she had a scarlet "A" tattooed across her face, even though adultery wasn't any of the things she and Wyatt were doing.

Once they were seated, a waiter scurried over and Wyatt ordered a bottle of wine. Maggie sat silently, her purse in her lap, feeling the heat in her face. Two other tables on the balcony were occupied, and Maggie felt like she'd walked in naked.

Once the waiter was gone, Wyatt looked at Maggie and sighed. "I'm sorry this is traumatizing you," he said quite seriously. "But you really are adorable when you blush like that."

"Wyatt, this isn't funny," Maggie said quietly.

"It's not meant to be," he said.

"We've talked about this," she said. "Two years until early retirement. They're gonna fire you."

"Maggie—" he started.

"When they find out—"

"Half of them already knew, Maggie," he said.

"What do you mean, 'knew'?"

"My meeting with the honchos. Most of them already knew about us," he said. "So much for hard and fast policy. Obviously they were okay with it as long as we weren't blatant about it."

"This is blatant, Wyatt!" Maggie said sharply, her voice just above a whisper. "They're going to be forced to fire you!"

"No, they're going to be forced to give me the transfer I asked for," he said.

Maggie felt like she'd been punched in the chest, but the waiter arrived with their wine, so she had no choice but to sit there silently while he decanted the wine and spouted off a number of appetizers and specials.

Maggie didn't even hear what Wyatt ordered, and missed out on taking his to task for ordering for her, which she would have done under different circumstances. When the waiter finally left, Maggie swallowed hard and managed to speak in a normal tone.

"Transfer to where?' she asked.

"Not to where, to what," Wyatt said. He picked up her wineglass and held it out to her. "Take a big drink of this."

Maggie took the glass and drained a good third of the wine.

"I've asked them to give me Karl's job," Wyatt said. "I asked them back in July, when I got shot. They turned me down."

Karl was the Sheriff's Office's public information officer. He was retiring in just two weeks.

Maggie leaned forward. "July? Why didn't you tell me that?" she whispered angrily at him.

"Because I wanted their answer first," he whispered back.

"Well, they said 'no,' Wyatt!"

"And now they'll reconsider," Wyatt said. "They're going to have to."

"You're not a public relations person!"

"Who cares, Maggie? It's a lateral move. I won't be your boss, and I'll still get my pension." He leaned even closer. "Meanwhile, if we keep hissing at each other like a couple of garter snakes, people are gonna say we're not only lovers, but we're having lovers' quarrels in public, and tomorrow morning everybody from the Mayor to your gynecologist will be talking about it. So I would appreciate it if you'd calm down or, I swear on my borked hip, I will lean over and lick your neck. *That*'ll give 'em a heads-up."

Maggie sat back in her chair, glancing around her for a moment. A few people were looking, but not all, and while some looked interested, no one looked exactly condemning.

"Now," Wyatt said. "I've ordered us food that I don't understand and that will probably cost an arm and a leg. Let's try to enjoy it."

Maggie stared at him. He stared back.

"What?" he asked.

"Wyatt, what are you doing?" she asked quietly.

"I'm taking action, Maggie," he said. "That's what men do."

"Why now? I mean, we're okay the way we are."

"No, we're not. I told you when we started this that I wasn't just pissing around," Wyatt said. "I'm forty-eight, not sixteen. I'm tired of skulking around and I'm tired of waiting. And no, I'm not talking about sex."

"Wyatt!"

He leaned over and whispered. "Sex!"

"What do you mean, you're tired of waiting?" Maggie asked. "It's only been a few months."

"Don't kid yourself, Maggie," he said gently. "I've been waiting almost six years for you to figure out we're not just buddies."

Maggie sat and stared at him, then took a drink of her wine, trying not to notice that her hand was shaking. It was almost six years ago that her divorce had become final.

"I realize that you've had some catching up to do," Wyatt said quietly. "But judging by some of the things that you've said to me, I'm guessing that you're almost there."

"Almost where?' Maggie asked, wishing she had the steady hands to pour more wine.

Wyatt got just a little agitated again, and leaned toward her. "Do you want me to say it? I'd rather do it privately, and I'd rather you say it first, but if you need me to lay it out for you I will, but then you'll probably piss yourself and we'll have a whole different gossip problem."

Maggie was trying to sort out seven possible responses when she saw the waiter approaching, and her eyes widened. Wyatt looked over his shoulder, then back at her.

"Try not to look like a gigged frog; the appetizers are here," he whispered.

"What is it?' she asked automatically.

"I don't remember," he said.

The waiter arrived at the table and put two plates down between them.

"I thought you might like to share these, so we'll just put them in the center," the waiter said cheerfully. "Can I get you anything else? More water?"

"No, thank you. This is great," Wyatt said distractedly.

When the waiter had gone, Wyatt reached over and poured them both some more wine. He handed Maggie her glass, then raised his own.

"Here's to the County Commissioners," he said.

Maggie looked at him, with his glass in the air, and got a sudden flash of Boudreaux earlier that day, raising his beer bottle to her. She got a sensation, like a small animal chewing at the back of her neck, but she couldn't put her finger on it. She felt that there was something else, something that refused to come out from around the edges of her mind.

She raised her glass, though she didn't raise it very high, for fear that everyone was looking.

TWENTY-ONE

Wyatt and Maggie, by some unspoken agreement, passed the rest of their meal engaged in little more than their usual chit-chat and banter. They both stayed away from talk of work, and they both stayed away from any more emotionally taxing topics.

They enjoyed their meal, but they didn't order more wine and they didn't linger. They were grown-ups, eating in public like grown-up couples do, but that didn't mean they had to dawdle over it.

Once they got outside, Wyatt unlocked the truck and opened Maggie's door. "As much as I would like us to go back to the house and do some kissing and maybe even break out that playlist, I think you need some time to toss things around in your head. So I'm just going to run you back to your car, okay?"

"Okay," Maggie said.

Wyatt ducked his head and gave her a quick kiss, and Maggie slid into the truck. She waited for Wyatt to close her door, but he didn't. He just stood there with his arm on it, jingling his keys.

"What?' she asked after a moment.

Wyatt frowned at her. "Something's wonky," he said.

"What's wonky?" she asked.

He shook his head, then looked over his shoulder down the street. "I don't know. The something-something isn't right."

They'd worked together long enough for Maggie to know he meant something with the case. "What?" she asked.

"I don't know," he said again, and shut her door.

She watched him walk around the front, and he got in and shut his door, still frowning. He put the key in the ignition, and stared at his steering wheel for a moment, then started up the truck.

"Let's just make a quick stop over on Water Street," he said as he backed out.

⚓   ⚓   ⚓

They got to the middle of the block, about half a block before Sea-Fair and, just beyond it, the building where Crawford's Seafood had been. Wyatt stopped in the middle of the empty street, and reached behind him to the small back seat.

He brought his copy of the case file to his lap, flipped through a couple of pages, then shut the file again and tossed it back on the seat.

"Yeah, this is where Fitch lived, this one over here," Wyatt said.

He pulled to the side of the road in front of a couple of small frame buildings.

"It was there," Wyatt said, pointing. "The one with the little porch."

The small house he was pointing at appeared to be a duplex. It had also been empty for a few years, Maggie knew. The yard had become overgrown, and there was a graying picket fence in front, but only half of one.

Wyatt shut off the truck, and they both got out. Wyatt looked around, then led the way onto the porch. Their footsteps seemed unusually loud in the silence of a block that saw little activity after business hours.

"Okay, so he's standing here on his porch, having his cigarette, and he looks down the street," Wyatt said, his hands on the porch rail.

"Clear shot," Maggie said.

"Yeah. Dark though, unless that light over Crawford's door was on," Wyatt said.

"Yeah. Still, a decent view."

"It bothers the crap out of me," Wyatt said, staring down the street.

"What does?"

"The car. The car bothers the crap out of me."

"Why?"

"I'm not sure," Wyatt answered. "So, he's smoking his cigarette, and he sees Crawford and the shorter guy out front, and raised voices, etcetera, he thinks they're arguing maybe."

Maggie was staring down the street as well. "Right."

"Then the other guy maybe punches Crawford, but probably stabs him," Wyatt said.

"Then the taller guy comes out front," Maggie said. "He seemed like he was rushing to help Crawford, to break up the fight."

"And we both figure that's Luedtke," Wyatt said.

"Do we know how tall Luedtke was?" Wyatt asked.

Maggie thought about the picture she'd seen, the men working for Bayside that summer. "Not as tall as my dad, so maybe six-feet?" she answered. "Tall, anyway."

"So Fitch goes back inside, and a couple minutes later, maybe less, he hears a car and looks outside," Wyatt said.

He put his hands on Maggie's shoulders and turned her around to face away from Crawford's. He turned around, too.

"So, he looks out his window," Wyatt said, and turned back around. So did Maggie. "What did he see?"

"He thought he saw Crawford driving away, but that's not very likely," Maggie said. "It was probably all three of them."

"Right," Wyatt said, distracted, as he stared down the street. "But it's wrong."

Maggie waited, looking down the street, letting Wyatt think.

"What were they doing here?" he asked finally.

"Well, we talked about Luedtke," Maggie said. "It's conceivable that he was working late."

"Yeah, but what was Crawford doing here?" Wyatt asked, finally looking at her.

Maggie looked back down the street, shrugged a little. "He came back to get his car," she said.

"Yeah, but why leave it here if you're going pubbing down the street? Then you have to walk all the way back."

Maggie looked back down the street. "The car is wrong."

"The car is wrong," Wyatt repeated, then he held up a finger and jogged down the steps and to the truck.

Maggie followed, as Wyatt opened the door and reached into the back seat to grab the file. He flipped through a couple of pages and then pulled out his cell phone and dialed. Maggie waited by the door.

"Hi, Mrs. Porter?" Wyatt asked. "This is Sheriff Hamilton. I'm fine, thank you. I'm sorry to bother you again, but I just have one more quick question. You said Mrs. Crawford got to the house around eight-thirty. Did somebody drop her off?" Wyatt looked up at Maggie as he listened. "And what kind of car was that? Okay, thank you, you've been great. Thanks."

Wyatt disconnected the call and looked at Maggie. "Crawford's car. Red Caprice."

"Mrs. Crawford said her car had died," Maggie said quietly. "She had Crawford's car."

Wyatt pointed down the street with his phone. "Which ended up there."

"Luedtke was here because she was here," Maggie said.

"And vice versa," Wyatt said. "I bet she told Crawford she went to the sister's a lot. But she was with Luedtke."

They both stared down the street a minute.

"But that's stupid to just leave the car right out front where he could see it," Wyatt said. "It would make sense for him to walk this way to go home. It's like three blocks. Why bother telling the husband she's going to her sister's—why bother going to the sister's—if you're just gonna leave the car sitting right out front?"

Maggie turned and looked at Wyatt. "No. She went to her sister's for the alibi," Maggie said, then looked back at the street.

"So Crawford comes by on his way home, sees his car. Steps inside, and what? Finds his wife baiting some other guy's hook—"

Maggie cut him off. "Here? At the plant? Not very romantic." She held Wyatt's eyes for a moment, watched him come to the same conclusion she had. "She wanted him to catch them."

Wyatt looked at her. "You think Luedtke knew that? If this was planned, they could have been a hell of a lot more discreet." He looked back down the street. "You think she set them both up? Forced a confrontation between the two of them so Luedtke would kill him?"

"Yeah," Maggie said, but it felt wrong, and she got that sensation at the back of her neck again, the one she'd gotten at dinner, when she'd remembered Boudreaux raising his drink to her.

"No," she said. "No, that's wrong, too."

TWENTY-TWO

The next morning was cool and dry, and there was a nice breeze over the manicured grounds of the Sunset Bay community.

Mrs. Crawford's nurse seemed surprised to see them without a call ahead from the main office. Mrs. Crawford seemed surprised, as well, when she opened the door to Maggie and Wyatt and Dwight.

"Well, hello," she said. She managed a smile for Wyatt, but it faltered a bit when she saw Dwight standing behind him.

"Hello, Mrs. Crawford," Wyatt said. "May we come in? We just have a few more questions."

"Well, yes," she answered, as she opened the door wider and stepped back. "But I do need to leave shortly. I have an appointment at the funeral home." She closed the door, looked nervously at Dwight, who nervously looked back, and then she brushed at a piece of lint on her black trousers.

"This shouldn't take too long, ma'am," Wyatt said. "Why don't we have a seat?"

"Sure. Of course," she said, and everyone but Dwight took a seat at the table. Dwight stayed by the door.

Maggie watched Mrs. Crawford, as the older woman glanced over at Dwight. It seemed to make her uncomfortable that Dwight was there, but not as uncomfortable as asking about his purpose might be.

"Mrs. Crawford, you mentioned the other day that your car had stopped running, that you were about to buy another one," Wyatt said. "Do you remember that?"

"Yes," she answered.

"How did you get to your sister's that night?"

Mrs. Crawford blinked at Wyatt a couple of times, but her face remained blank. "Oh, well, I got a ride from a friend," she answered. She fiddled with her hair a bit. "I can't remember who."

"According to your sister's nurse, you were driving your husband's car," Maggie said.

"What?" The old woman tugged at her earlobe. "I—wait, yes, I think I remember now. Holden dropped me off, and then my friend—goodness, what was her name?—she took me back home later on."

"No, that's not right, Mrs. Crawford," Wyatt said. "Mrs. Porter said your husband's car was still in your sister's driveway when she left at nine. At nine, your husband was at Papa Joe's."

"I don't understand what you're saying," Mrs. Crawford said. "I'm getting confused."

"You were driving your husband's car," Wyatt said patiently. "Which was parked at your husband's place of business when he was last seen around ten, arguing with two people out front."

Mrs. Crawford didn't respond, just stared at Wyatt like he was speaking in tongues.

"You were there with Terry Luedtke, isn't that right, Mrs. Crawford?" Maggie asked.

The woman looked at her. "What?"

"Terry Luedtke. He didn't just start having feelings for you sometime after your husband's disappearance, did he?" Maggie asked.

Now it was Maggie's turn to get blinked at.

"You were having an affair with Luedtke," Maggie said. "Did you know they found an engagement ring in his personal effects, Mrs. Crawford?"

The woman's lips pursed a few times. "I don't— you don't understand," she said.

"What would you like us to understand, ma'am?" Wyatt asked.

"I was—it was terrifying," she said.

"What was?" Wyatt asked her.

"Yes. Yes, I was seeing Terry. I'm so sorry," she said, her voice rising. "I didn't know he would do anything to Holden."

"So you and Terry were there and your husband showed up and caught you?" Wyatt asked. "Is that what you're saying? And Terry stabbed your husband."

"Yes! Mrs. Crawford put a palm to her mouth. "It was awful. It was so fast."

The apartment door opened, and the nurse stepped in, glanced at Dwight and then at the group at the table.

"Is everything all right in here?"

"Oh, Jeanette!" Mrs. Crawford cried out.

The nurse frowned at Wyatt and Maggie, then hurried to Mrs. Crawford's side. "What is going on?" she asked Wyatt.

"We're just clearing some things up with Mrs. Crawford," Wyatt said.

Maggie pulled the picture of the men from Bayside Construction out of her purse and laid it on the table in front of Mrs. Crawford. The woman glanced at it without seeming to see it, as Maggie pulled a pen out of her purse and set it next to the picture.

"Mrs. Crawford, would you be so kind as to draw a circle around Terry Luedtke?"

"What?" Mrs. Crawford leaned in to take a closer look.

"Could you just draw a circle around his head for us? Which one is he?"

"Oh, yes."

She picked up the pen and looked at the picture. Maggie could tell when her eyes found Luedtke, smiling shyly and raising his beer. Mrs. Crawford's eyes flickered just a little. Her hand trembled as she drew a small red circle around his face. Then she looked up at Wyatt.

"I didn't know he would hurt Holden," she said. "It all happened so quickly, and I didn't know what to do. I was afraid he'd hurt me, too, if I didn't help him."

"That's a lot of crap, Mrs. Crawford," Maggie said. "Luedtke didn't kill your husband."

"Hey, now," the nurse said.

Maggie ignored her. "Luedtke didn't kill your husband," she said to Mrs. Crawford. "Your husband was almost six-three. And, yeah, next to a six-foot-three guy in work boots, even a five-foot-nine woman will look like 'a shorter guy'—which is how Fitch described you."

"What?" Mrs. Crawford asked, nervously clicking the pen over and over again. "You're confusing me, I don't understand what you're talking about."

"Save the Betty White impression for court, Mrs. Crawford," Maggie said.

"Mrs. Crawford isn't well," the nurse said. "She has Alzheimer's."

I'm sure she's earned it," Maggie said, then looked back at Mrs. Crawford, who was still holding the red pen in her left hand. Maggie held up the picture. "The person who stabbed your husband was left-handed, Mrs. Crawford. Terry Luedtke—" here she pointed to Luedtke, forever holding that beer aloft "—wasn't."

Mrs. Crawford set the pen down on the table, looked over at Wyatt and then up at her nurse. "I'm so confused. I don't remember," she said.

"Maybe it'll come back to you," Maggie said. "Oh, wait. I hear it usually doesn't."

The next morning was bright and clear, and Maggie squinted against the sun, even with her sunglasses, as she walked up the steps of Boudreaux's front porch and knocked on the door.

Amelia opened the door and looked at Maggie blankly. "Mr. Bennett round back foolin' with his mangos," she said.

Maggie nodded for no particular reason, since Amelia had already shut the door, albeit quietly.

Maggie walked around the porch, her hiking boots thumping against the wide planks. Once she rounded the corner, she saw Boudreaux, in loose khaki pants and a blue chambray shirt, pulling yellow leaves from a small potted mango tree.

She walked down the back steps, and Boudreaux looked up as she approached. For once, he seemed surprised to see her.

"Good morning, Maggie," he said.

"Mr. Boudreaux."

"I'm just trying to help this one become a little more enthusiastic about surviving," he said.

Boudreaux had more than a dozen full-sized mango trees, and several more potted ones, of many varieties. They did very well, despite the fact that Apalach was generally too far north for mangos. He spent a lot of money on heaters and greenhouses and tarps to make that happen, and Maggie knew he did it all for Miss Evangeline.

Boudreaux tossed the yellow leaves to the grass and wiped his hands on his pants. "It's an unusual pleasure to see you here, Maggie," he said.

"I just have a few minutes," she said.

"Let's go up on the porch," he said. "Amelia just brought out some fresh Indian River grapefruit juice."

He gestured for her to go ahead of him, and she almost said she didn't have time, but she skipped it. It seemed to be a routine for them, either oysters or a beverage.

She walked back up to the porch and he followed her, then led the way to a small table and chairs, where a pitcher of deep red juice sat sweating.

Maggie sat down as Boudreaux took a couple of glasses from the small bar and brought them to the table. She watched him as he sat down and poured their juice. Then she took a sip before she looked back up at him. He was waiting, as he always did, those eyes going right through her.

"I just wanted to let you know that the Crawford case has been wrapped up," she said. "Without you."

"So I hear," he said. Maggie sighed at him. "People like to tell me things."

Maggie nodded and watched him take a sip of his juice.

"I was surprised to hear about Mrs. Crawford," he said. "She didn't seem the type. Maybe I'm not as perceptive as I think."

"One of the things I don't like about my job is that people still surprise me," Maggie said. "The ugliness in people."

He watched her for a moment, and she worried that she might have offended him. She hadn't actually thought of him, or the things he'd done or been rumored to have done, when she'd said it.

"Why did you go to work for the Sheriff's Office, Maggie? It doesn't seem to make you particularly happy."

"Sometimes it does," she said. "When I can actually help someone."

"Was it because of your grandfather?"

Maggie thought about that for a moment. "I'm sure it was partly that, and partly that I knew my parents didn't have the money for law school, even though they said they could swing it," she said.

Boudreaux scratched at his eyebrow for a moment.

"I think it was also because I was afraid," she said, and was surprised she said it.

"Really," Boudreaux said, quietly. "Afraid of what?"

Maggie looked over at him and wondered why it was so easy to talk to him about things that were hard for her to talk about. In some respects, this relationship she shouldn't be having was more comfortable than most.

"Everything," she said.

Boudreaux stared at her for a moment. His eyes were piercing still, but there was kindness there, too. She'd seen it before.

"I've seen you act with a great deal of bravery, Maggie," he said.

Maggie began to feel too inspected, and she looked out into the yard.

"But bravery isn't the absence of fear, is it?" she asked. "It's doing something regardless of fear, don't you think?"

"Yes. I think that's true."

She looked back at him. "I think when something truly bad happens to you, something really scary, the knowledge never leaves you—the knowledge that bad things don't just happen to other people. So it's easy to be scared that they will happen."

He stared at her, but said nothing. He reminded her of therapists on TV.

"It's made me a bit of a paranoid mother," Maggie said, and tried to smile.

"You're a police officer," Boudreaux said. "Even without what happened to you as a teenager, you'd have plenty of good reasons to fear for your children. In any event, we're all afraid of something."

"I suppose," Maggie said. "What are you afraid of, Mr. Boudreaux?"

He idly rubbed at the edge of one eyebrow for a moment, then smiled at her. "I'm afraid of Miss Evangeline."

She sort of smiled back. "Worried about the voodoo?"

"I once watched her stand up to my father," he said. "The voodoo is far less frightening."

Maggie took another sip of her juice, and her smile slowly faded. "Was my father your alibi, Mr. Boudreaux?"

He actually seemed surprised by that question. He put down his own glass. "No, he wasn't."

"Are you going to tell me who was?"

"No, I'm not."

Maggie nodded, then stood up. "Well, I need to go."

Boudreaux stood with her. "So soon?"

"I have to wrap up some paperwork, then I have a date with my dad," she said. "We're taking the kids out on the boat this afternoon."

He nodded. "Well, I hope you have a good day," he said.

She took the hand he held out, felt the old oystering callouses, felt the gentle squeeze before she let go.

"You, too, Mr. Boudreaux," she said, then turned and headed back the way she'd come. When she rounded the corner, she looked back. He was still watching her, his hands in his pockets.

He really was a very interesting man.

⚓ ⚓ ⚓

A few hours later, Boudreaux was sitting in one of the Adirondack chairs in the back yard, immersed in his favorite Faulkner, when he heard footsteps on the pavers.

He looked up, and she was standing there, the breeze brushing her long dark hair across her cheek.

"Hello," she said, and there was a touch of discomfort in her green eyes.

He stood up, dropped his book down on the small table beside his chair.

"Hello, Mrs. Redmond," he said politely.

"I'm sorry to disturb you," she said. "The woman who answered the door said you were back here."

"It's quite all right," he said, then he waited. He had no desire to make her feel uncomfortable, but he really wasn't quite sure what he should say.

"I just wanted to say thank you," she said finally.

"For what?" he asked.

"For not saying anything," she answered. "Although, I would have had to say something if this thing hadn't been cleared up."

"It wasn't necessary," he said.

She looked away, toward the mango trees, and caught the corner of her lower lip in her teeth. He thought, not for the first time, how much alike mother and daughter were.

"I would have had to do the right thing," she said without looking at him. "I tried to do the right thing then."

"So I heard," he said. "I appreciate that, but it seems Sheriff Bradford had more loyalty to your father than he did to the law."

She looked at him. "I'm sorry. Cops look out for each other. When they can."

"Yes," he said. "Nevertheless, it worked itself out."

They looked at each other for a moment, and he remembered how she'd looked that night, so pretty and fresh and sad, so uncertain about a future married to her high school sweetheart. So lonely looking, standing there alone on the seawall where Riverfront Park was now.

It had started as a moderately chivalric desire to make sure she was all right, but then there'd gradually been less chivalry. He had wondered what it would be like to be with a good girl, and she had wondered what it would be like to be less good. He liked to think he wouldn't have gone through with it if he'd known she was a virgin.

"Gray says that we're going to need to tell her one day soon," she said. She tried to smile, then looked away. "He thinks she'll forgive us eventually."

"He knows her well," Boudreaux said. "He might be right."

She gave a short laugh that had no humor in it. "She might eventually forgive me for what I did, but she'll forgive Gray for lying to her all these years a whole lot faster. She's her daddy's girl, and I don't mean that in a bitter way. She just is."

Boudreaux swallowed, and worked at not having any expression at all on his face.

"Yes, she is," he said.

She looked him in the eye then, and seemed to realize what she'd said. She opened her mouth as though to apologize, then shut it again. She looked away, but not before a tear fell from the corner of one eye.

"Are you all right, Mrs. Redmond?" he asked.

She looked back at him and smiled one of those smiles that women fake to look like they're just fine.

"Yes. Thank you," she said. "I need to go."

"Thank you for coming by," he said.

She nodded, then turned and walked away.

He watched her go, her gait so familiar to him, but only because it was Maggie's. She'd meant nothing to him then, and he was ashamed to admit that she meant nothing to him now. But he did admire the way she loved his daughter.

⚓ ⚓ ⚓

Maggie stood in the stern of her father's little twenty-footer, dumping more ice into the cooler to cover Sky's decent-sized redfish.

Her sunglasses fell off of her face into the cooler, and she reached down and picked them up, then straightened up and wiped them on her shirt as she squinted over at her father.

Daddy was hunched over, deep in conversation with Kyle as they baited his hook. She couldn't help but be reminded of similar trips years ago, and Daddy helping David with his line.

She put her sunglasses back on, passed behind Sky where she was standing at the portside rail, and sat back down on one of the cushioned gear boxes. She watched as her father clapped Kyle on the back and watched him cast his line.

She was still fairly certain that Boudreaux had told her some kind of half-truth about why he'd met her father that day on Lafayette Pier. She was also fairly certain that her father would tell her the same, or another, half-truth if she asked him about it.

She had trusted her father implicitly all of her life. Not once had she ever questioned his honesty. Nor had she ever doubted his love. If she questioned him about Boudreaux, he would be hurt, and maybe she would force him to lie. It would hurt him even more if he knew that she had begun to wonder about his involvement thirty-eight years ago, deep down in some place that even she had barely acknowledged.

As a rule, she didn't believe in fathers and daughters keeping secrets from each other, but as he looked over his shoulder and smiled at her, his sandy hair blowing in the breeze, she decided that she would let these two secrets, his and hers, slip into the past untold.

AUTHOR'S NOTE

Thank you so much for spending a little bit of your time in Apalach. You are deeply appreciated.

If you've missed any of the previous books in the series, you can find them all at,

amazon.com/gp/product/B014F6NT48/

If you'd like to be the first to know when the next book in the series is released, please like my page on Facebook,

fb.com/Dawn-Lee-McKenna-147050526

or you can sign up for my newsletter here.

dawnleemckenna.com

Subscribers always have the opportunity to get new releases for just 99 cents.

You can also feel free to drop me a line at dawnmckenna63@gmail.com. Hearing from you guys is one of the highlights of my day. Some days, that's not saying much, but I trust you to get the sentiment.

If you can spare a few more minutes of your day, I'd appreciate you leaving a review on Amazon.

Look for the next release in the Forgotten Coast series by mid-February 2016, and keep an eye out for the launch of my new series, featuring Wyatt's friend Evan Caldwell, at some point in the not-too- distant future. There's no rooster, but there is a cat.

Made in the USA
Middletown, DE
20 July 2016